ex Lib

50

W9-BBO-094

WATSONVILLE COMMUNITY HOSPITAL
298 GREEN VALLEY ROAD
WATSONVILLE, CA 95076

00911

1900

DEATH
FROM THE
LADIES' TEE

Previous Hacker mystery by James Y. Bartlett

Death Is a Two-Stroke Penalty

DEATH
FROM THE
LADIES' TEE

A HACKER MYSTERY

JAMES Y. BARTLETT

St. Martin's Press   New York

DEATH FROM THE LADIES' TEE. Copyright © 1992 by James Y. Bartlett. All rights reserved. Printed in the United States of America. No part of this book may be used or reproduced in any manner whatsoever without written permission except in the case of brief quotations embodied in critical articles or reviews. For information, address St. Martin's Press, 175 Fifth Avenue, New York, N.Y. 10010.

Design by Tanya Pérez

Library of Congress Cataloging-in-Publication Data

Bartlett, James Y.
   Death from the ladies' tee : A Hacker mystery / James Y. Bartlett.
      p.   cm.
   "A Thomas Dunne book."
   ISBN 0-312-07699-1
   I. Title.
   PS3552.A76539D38   1992
   813'.54—dc20   92-3019
                                                                   CIP

First edition: June 1992

10 9 8 7 6 5 4 3 2 1

TO MY MOTHER

AND TO HER SISTERS, ALL OF WHOM HAVE MANAGED THEIR LIVES,
AND GOLF GAMES, WITH GRACE AND STYLE, UNFLAGGING GOOD
HUMOR, AND BOUNDLESS ENTHUSIASM

THREE THINGS THERE ARE AS UNFATHOMABLE AS THEY ARE
FASCINATING TO THE MASCULINE MIND: METAPHYSICS; GOLF;
AND THE FEMININE HEART.

—ARNOLD HAULTAIN, *THE MYSTERY OF GOLF*

GOLF MAY BE A SOPHISTICATED GAME. AT LEAST, IT IS USUALLY
PLAYED WITH THE OUTWARD APPEARANCE OF GREAT DIGNITY.
IT IS, NEVERTHELESS, A GAME OF CONSIDERABLE PASSION,
EITHER OF THE EXPLOSIVE TYPE, OR THAT WHICH BURNS
INWARDLY AND SEARS THE SOUL.

—BOB JONES

DEATH
FROM THE
LADIES' TEE

CHAPTER 1

S on-of-a-bitchin' mother-fuck-in' goddam' shit-eatin' puke!"

I am ashamed to say that those were the first words my new neighbor heard me utter. It was a gloriously warm and sunny day in late April on Boston's North Shore, and I scored a direct hit, hammer upon thumb, just as the tall and somewhat gangly woman strode confidently around the corner of my beach shack.

I performed a cartoonesque dance of pain, leaping about furiously, shaking the throbbing digit, then cramming it into my mouth for a soothing suck, until I finally noticed her standing there. Her eyes had widened perceptibly. Her lips were pursed in something of a smile.

"Oh, dear," she said, trying not to laugh. "I should expect that would smart." Her voice was clipped just this side of pseudo-British. Her mousy brown hair was pulled back off her face and tied in a proper bun. She was, as I said, tall and rather gangly, with broad shoulders and long, thin arms and legs. Although thin, she was still properly curved. She wore a

1

sleeveless blouse and shorts, but had a sensible cable-knit sweater knotted around her shoulders. I try hard not to type-cast people, but I immediately registered, "Cambridge . . . professor . . . spinster-to-be."

" 'Scuse me," I mumbled, thumb still in mouth.

"Quite all right, done it many a time myself," she said forcefully. She reached out, grabbed my unhurt hand, and began pumping it up and down.

"Moira Daughtry," she said. "My friends call me 'Mo.' We're to be neighbors this summer. Here, let me."

She picked my hammer up from where I had dropped it, steadied the shutter I had been holding, and drove the nail home with one firm blow, securing the shutter in place.

It was my vacation. I always take the better part of a month off in late April and early May. Exactly one week ago, I had been in Augusta to witness "the Dashing Scot," Ian MacDuff, capture the hallowed Masters with a sterling back nine, another historic Sunday afternoon in Augusta. Because there are no really important tournaments immediately after the Masters, my editor agrees to give me time off. I would pick up the Tour again in mid-May, as the golfers began to raise their intensity in preparation for June's U.S. Open.

As I do every year, I was spending my time trying to get my beach house in shape for the season. It's not much of a house, but it's one of my most treasured possessions. It had belonged to my Uncle Charles, a dedicated and lifelong bachelor and globe-trotting oil company executive who had left the house to me to use as he had: as a brief but total respite from the ordinary world.

The house is located on an isolated spit of land called Cross Banks overlooking Ipswich Bay, about thirty-five miles north of Boston. There are maybe a dozen shacks like mine on this bluff, protected at the rear by a few hundred acres of marsh-land. From our narrow strip, the dunes run down to a rocky beach. As you face the bay, off to the left is the Plum Island bird sanctuary, and across a broad tidal cut to the right is Crane's Beach.

Uncle Charley had not been able to use the house any more

2

frequently than I managed to now. I like to spend my few spring weeks at the house, repairing winter damage, preparing for the summer onslaught, and enjoying the peace and quiet and emptiness of the place. And I try to escape for a week in September, when the crowds go back home, and the golden tones of the early fall sun wash the gloriously clean and empty beaches. During the summer, when I am busy chronicling the victories and defeats of the PGA Tour, various relatives sign up for week-long visits; I rent the place out, only to those I know well, the rest of the time. I don't know how they stand it: It's a tiny place, two bedrooms, bath, kitchenette, living room, and deck facing the sea. More than enough for just me, but it must be hideously cramped, noisy, and smelly for the families-with-children who pile in.

Anyway, the neighborly Mo Daughtry finished nailing up the shutter supports along the south wall with professional aplomb. While I nursed my thumb, she chattered all the while about her adjacent shack, which she was renting from a very good friend in the English Department for the summer, how much she admired the view, and how she hoped before summer's end to stage a genuine New England clambake down on the beach and would I like to help?

I explained gently to her that I would only be on site for a week or three.

I could see her face fall. She had apparently been measuring me out for a relationship suit.

"And what is your occupation, er, Mister . . . ?" she asked graciously.

"Hacker. Pete Hacker. I write for the *Boston Journal,*" I said.

"Ahhh, a journalist," she exclaimed, her eyes brightening again. I could see her mental tape measure come slinging out again.

"Well, not quite," I said. "I'm a sportswriter. I cover the professional golf tour."

"Ah," she said, eyes clouding again. Then she brightened. This woman was determined. "My uncle played golf," she

3

ventured, in an effort to keep our conversation going. "Winston Butterfield was his name. Do you know of him?"

"Gosh, you know, I don't think I do," I said. "Of course, there are only twenty-five million golfers in this country, so maybe I just haven't gotten around to meeting him yet." Okay, I sounded a little peevish. But this damn woman was beginning to irritate me. I come to the beach to get away from people, not to socialize. Although she did wield a pretty good hammer.

Anyway, she got my drift.

"Of course," she said. "How silly of me. Well, it has been a pleasure meeting you. I hope to see you and Mrs. Hacker again soon."

"There is no Mrs. Hacker," I told her.

"Ah," she said, eyes alight again. "Well then, toodle-oo!" She disappeared around the side of my house in a jaunty, loose-limbed gait. Toodle-oo. I don't think anyone had ever actually said that to me before in my entire life. Toodle-oo.

I got the cold sweats thinking about it.

CHAPTER 2

I wisely decided to postpone the rest of my planned renovation activities until the next day. The shutter project and the new screen for the front door could wait until Monday.

There were maybe two good hours of sun left in the afternoon, and in Boston in late April one learns to treasure warm sun. It does not last. I threw on an old sweater, poured myself a healthy Dewar's on the rocks, grabbed a thick book on English history, and went out to the deck. I figured to use the sweater and the Scotch to scientifically counteract the steady diminution of the sun's warmth as it set behind me. After an hour or so, I got up and refilled the glass. A line of low, scudding clouds had blown up and I could feel the temperature begin to drop. Tomorrow looked to be cloudy and cool with a chance of rain. "Darn," I thought, facetiously, "might have to postpone those damn shutters another day."

My telephone rang just as I had decided to call it an afternoon. I went inside and answered it.

"Hacker, is that you?" a cheerful female voice asked. "God, I can't believe what a pain in the ass it has been to track you down. You'll never guess who this is!" The voice giggled happily.

She was young, I could tell, and sounded vaguely familiar. "I give up," I said.

"Honie Carlton!" she exclaimed. "Remember me?"

I immediately felt old. I think five more of my hairs turned grey in that instant. Honie Carlton had been a neighbor child back home in Wallingford. When I had left home to seek fame and fortune, she had been barely in her teens, the girl who lived a few houses down. Over the years, she and my parents had become close. They took an interest in her, and she adopted them. Baked goods and gossip passed across the fence developed into an abiding love. I would always hear about her progress in school on my intermittent visits home. At Thanksgiving or Christmas she would sometimes drop in for a dram of holiday cheer. A pretty young thing, every year growing in female gracefulness. Last report I had heard, a few years ago, was that she was in college now, studying marketing.

"Honie Carlton," I said. "You sound all growed up. How *did* you find me?"

She laughed—a clear, self-satisfied, tinkling laugh.

"Well, I started by calling New Orleans, where I thought you'd be with the Tour," she said. "I talked to some guy down there named Corcoran, who said he didn't know where in the hell you were."

"That's Billy, the information officer," I said. "You should have talked to his assistant, gal named Suzy. She knows more than he ever forgot, which is a lot."

"Well, then I called the sports desk at the *Journal*, but whoever answered said you were probably down in New Orleans, ummm, 'banging some golf groupies' was the way he put it, I think." She laughed again.

I was too embarrassed to respond. The Honie of memory had been such an innocent, clean-cut child.

"Then, I did what I shoulda done first," she continued. "I called your old man. He said you were on vacation and probably out fixing up your beach shack. And here you are!"

"Well damn, you deserve the gold medal in perseverance," I said. "What are you up to these days?"

"I graduated from college in December," she said, "and after looking around and interviewing all over the damn place, I got a job two months ago."

"Which is . . ."

"Information officer for the Ladies' Professional Golf Tour," she said.

"Aha," I said.

"Oh, Hacker, now don't be that way," she gushed. "I'm not calling to hustle you. Well, I guess I am in a way, but not . . ."

She laughed again, self-consciously this time.

I chuckled. "I'm just yanking your chain, kid," I said. "Congratulations, that's a great job, especially for a young kid like you. And God knows they need the help."

The LPGA, though more than forty years old, had fallen upon somewhat hard times. It was having problems attracting fans, sponsors, and television coverage, and no one was quite sure why.

"But didn't I hear that your degree was in marketing?" I asked.

"Yeah, this is kind of the first step," Honie said. "You see, what this tour needs is marketing and exposure. I'm working the exposure end right now, and I'm in line to move into marketing in a year or two."

"I didn't know you were a golfer," I said.

"Oh hell, Hacker," she laughed, "I don't know a three-wood from a sand wedge. But my job isn't to play the silly game, just to get it into the public's mind."

"And how are you doing?" I asked, knowing I shouldn't.

"Well," she said coyly, "that's one reason I'm calling."

"The other being you just had to catch up on old news from an old someone you remember hardly at all," I chided.

"You're right, Hacker." She laughed. "Business is business. But you're the best golf writer I know . . . hell, the only golf writer I know . . . and I thought, at the least, I could get some advice . . ." She trailed off hopefully.

7

"Put out plenty of cold beer and free cold cuts," I said. "They'll come flocking to do your bidding."

"Hacker," she said, and then laughed. "Seriously, we don't get much important news coverage, for some reason. I mean, *Golf World* usually has someone at the tournaments, and the AP and the local press usually do a pretty good job. But there's just no consistent national coverage, not even from the wire services, and I just don't know why. These girls can really play the game."

"I don't know why, either," I said. "At first blush, you'd just say the great American public doesn't go for women's professional sports. But then you think about tennis, and the women there seem to be able to pack 'em in okay. Of course, they play their major tournaments at the same time as the men, so they get built-in media exposure, which helps."

"Exposure is the key," Honie agreed. "We're trying real hard to get more tournaments on TV, but in the meantime, I've got to try and recruit some more print media attention. Which is why I thought of you," she said primly.

"Honie—" I started.

"I mean, you're not busy with the men's Tour right now . . ."

"Honie—"

"And we're in the middle of our Florida swing, and the weather's real nice down here . . ."

"Honie—"

"And it would really make me some Brownie points with my boss . . ."

"Honie—"

"And I can get you a free hotel room and interviews with anyone you want. We've got a real good field this week, and . . ."

"Honie—"

"What do you think? Will you come down?"

I used to think they taught Persistence 101 to women in college. But now I am beginning to believe that it's a natural, inborn trait of the species.

"Honie, it's my time off," I said gently. "I don't want to work. I want to putter around here and bang up my thumb

8

and read six good books I've been saving, and drink a lot of Scotch and watch the waves crash against the rocks over there and . . ." I stopped because I think I was beginning to whine a little. That's not good. It shows weakness. Women like weakness and know how to exploit it.

"Oh, that's all right, Hacker," Honie said. "I just thought you might like to spend a week down here in Miami. Did I mention that we're playing at the Doral this weekend? I could get you a suite, I think. But if you'd rather not, I understand, I guess." She tried, unsuccessfully, to keep the disappointment out of her voice.

The great golfer Bob Jones used to say he believed that the results of every tournament he ever played were determined by some great Divine Providence before anyone teed off, and that all he and his competitors were doing was playing out the Will of said Providence.

I think Divine Providence must have wanted me in Miami, because just at that moment, I saw Mo Daughtry come striding toward the front door of the cottage. In the fading twilight, I saw that she carried a bottle of something, sherry, I guessed, and two glasses.

"Yoo-hoo, Peter!" she chirruped from the door. "I find myself in need of a corkscrew! Have you one handy?"

The yoo-hoo got me. So did the Peter. No one called me Peter. But so did the sudden clarity with which I saw my predicament. The two glasses were the tip-off. My corkscrew would lead to her offer of a neighborly sherry in thanks. And then two or three more. Followed by the batted eyes, the casual caress, and the shy giggles that would hopefully lead to a more serious and meaningful look. A hot, slack mouth suddenly attacking, hoping that the three, or maybe four, sherries would have broken down any remaining inhibitions. The frantic shedding of clothes, the unveiling of that rangy, knobby body, all sharp angles and bony joints, all pale white desperation. But with the sherry in you, who cares? And then the rushing, gasping, frantic chase, faster and faster. Bony hips digging into thighs. Release, collapse, oblivion. Until the morning, when we'd have to sort out the emotions and deter-

9

mine the level of commitment in the cold, harsh, unsherried light of daybreak.

And even if I was able to somehow avoid that scenario this night, tomorrow would bring another attack, a different strategy.

"Honie," I said into the phone. "I've changed my mind. Miami sounds great. I'll be down tomorrow afternoon."

"Oh, Hacker, thanks!" she exclaimed. "You are a prince! There's a flight from Boston at two P.M., gets in at four-thirty. I'll meet you."

I thought about that for a second. "How did you know what time the flights were?" I asked. "That's . . . that's . . ." I cast about for just the right expletive to hurl across the telephone line.

"Professional," she said. "Very professional."

CHAPTER 3

O n the plane ride down to
Miami the next afternoon,
I thought about the LPGA. It was true that the ladies' game
did not receive the same attention as the men's. Except for the
one week every summer when the women played a tournament
in Boston, news about their weekly tournaments was often
buried deep inside the *Boston Journal*'s sports section, right
next to the bowling league scores.

Something just didn't add up right. The women's professional tour had been around since the 1940s, and there had
been a steady succession of excellent women players over the
years: Babe Didrickson, Patty Berg, Mickey Wright, Kathy
Whitworth, JoAnne Carner, Wynnona Stilwell and, in recent
years, Nancy Lopez, Pat Bradley, Betsy King, Beth Daniel,
Patty Sheehan, and many others.

No, the marquee *names* were there. And so was the base of
fans. I had recently read some statistics that showed the number of women golfers in the United States had reached more
than twenty-five percent of the total of twenty-one million
golfers and was climbing steadily every year.

But the LPGA was struggling. The men's Senior Tour, that grayed and paunchy group of PGA stars from the recent past, had been organized just a few years ago and had rocketed to instant success: big purses, lots of tournaments, lots of sponsors, lots of TV coverage. And lots of fans. The LPGA had quickly and literally become the weak sister of professional golf, left to pick up the spoils that remained from the two men's tours.

Why was the LPGA having so much trouble attracting attention and dollars? The modern era of the Tour had been plagued by a series of terrible leaders whose mismanagement had saddled the organization with some heavy credibility problems among the powers that be, both at the networks and at the high corporate levels. And it was widely believed that women professionals, even on shortened golf courses, don't make enough birdies to attract a fan's interest. This, I knew, was a subjective opinion, but it held more than a grain of truth. While women professional golfers have the ability to move the ball, the women's game does not usually contain the same kind of bravura, knock-down-the-pins performance witnessed every week on the men's Tour. At least that's the common perception.

Further, I mused as the plane throbbed its way south over an unending bank of blue-gray clouds, the current women's tour did not seem to have developed a lot of distinctive personalities at the top. I cringed in my airplane seat as imaginary shrews shrieked their protests at me. *What about Betsy King?* they yelled. *Nancy Lopez? Beth Daniel? Pat Bradley? How can you say such a thing?*

I could say it because it was mostly true. Nancy Lopez certainly excited lots of attention back in her heyday, especially in 1978, the year she won five in a row. But these days, with three babies in tow, Nancy Lopez's best golf is behind her. Betsy King? A dominating player, but about as exciting as Swiss cheese. Beth Daniel? Ditto. Pat Bradley? Big, brawny, and powerful . . . but those are not adjectives of femininity that usually appeal to the admittedly sexist American public. Jan

Stephenson? Has the sex appeal Bradley and others lack, but not the golf game.

And so on. The bottom-line truth is that the LPGA was and is a public-relations disaster. And then there was the "image problem." There had always been whispering about the tour's so-called image problem. My more cynical golf-writer friends had a different phrase for it: "dykes in spikes."

To be sure, there are not a lot of soft, feminine-looking women playing at the top levels of the LPGA, but just how many of the players are lesbians is not known. The sexual inclination of the golfer is not included in her official press biography. But whenever the subject comes up in late-night, booze-fueled discussions among golf writers, and probably golf fans as well, the stories and the rumors and the conjectures go on and on. There's the winner of three major tournaments whose constant travel companion gets a decidedly nonsisterly kiss after every good round. The leading money winner who likes to cruise the leather bars in each city she visits. The new young players who are treated like "fresh meat" by the older, more experienced touring pros.

I had listened to, laughed at, and clucked over all these stories over the years. And while it never particularly mattered to me who was sleeping with whom, it figured that some element of homophobia was no doubt a factor in the LPGA's lack of marketing success. I thought of Laura Baugh and Jan Stephenson. Both players had been seized upon as "marketable" by the LPGA in large part because of their physical attractiveness: slim, trim, and blond. The heterosexual ideal.

I saw, in my mind's eye, the shape and substance of the kind of article I could get out of my weekend trip. It seemed to be more appropriate for the Sunday magazine section, I thought, and made a mental note to put in a call to the editor to discuss it with him. The readers of the *Journal*'s sports section are more comfortable with Red Sox box scores and some in-depth reportage on Wade Boggs's love life.

Honie Carlton was waiting for me when I deplaned in the humidity of Miami. I almost didn't recognize her. She had indeed grown up. The pert and cheerful little teen I remembered had become a stunning young woman, with all the requisite curves and shapes that entails. She wore a soft pink sleeveless top and a shapely white skirt. Her light brown hair was pulled back from her face and tied with a pink bow, and some cheerfully colored earrings jiggled with the movement of her head. Her pale blue eyes were alight in that perfect face, her soft round lips tinged with just the slightest shade of pink.

Like any other red-blooded American male, I felt my heart do some quick gonadal flip-flops as I studied her. But when I imagined what my mother would say about such thoughts concerning her surrogate daughter, I pushed them aside.

"Hacker!" she cried, coming up and giving me a chaste little kiss. "Jeez, it's good to see you. Thanks so much for coming."

"God, child, you make me feel old before my time," I replied, slinging my leather carryall over my shoulder and trying not to walk as stooped over as I felt. She frowned at me, prettily.

"When people say things like that to me, it makes me feel like I'm just fourteen and trying on my first training bra," she said, pouting.

"You're right," I said. "I apologize. It's always difficult for one generation to admit the next to all the privileges of adulthood."

"Whoa, that's deep." She giggled.

Making small talk, we collected my bags, walked outside into a thick vapor barrier of humidity, and piled into a cab.

Miami is probably my least favorite city in probably my least favorite state. Never mind the constant heat that always saps whatever reserves of strength I have built up; never mind the little bugs that seem to find me, no matter how far indoors I take myself or how thickly I lather myself with dope; never mind that the golf courses—uniformly flat, watery, and breezy—all seem to run together in my head after a while.

No, what I don't like about Miami, and Florida in general, is its built-in isolation. There are no neighborhoods in Miami, only walled compounds. Except for the slums and barrios. There are no houses with yards in Miami, just impregnable villas surrounded by high barriers and screened-in swimming

14

pools. Miami, the sun-and-fun capital of the world, is really an indoor place: hidden, private, secret. Air-conditioned and kept cool and dark. Protected by gatehouses and security guards and dog patrols and DO NOT ENTER signs.

Maybe they've got it right, and the rest of us are wrong. The world *is* a tough place: Carving out your private and hidden sanctuary and not letting anyone in without clearance is perhaps the way to combat that toughness. But as an outsider, Miami always makes me feel uneasy. A trespasser in paradise.

From the airport, our cab took us past a few of those walled paradises and through a few of Miami's many squalid slums before pulling swiftly through the enormous stucco wall that surrounds the very posh and private Doral Hotel and Country Club. We moved from the hot and humid and noisy street into a whisper-quiet, lushly landscaped tropical setting, with towering royal palms, expansively huge banana trees, flowering hibiscus and oleander, and acres of well-tended beds of coleus and marigold. Fountains gushed from lakes. A strong, athletic girl in a swimsuit of spun gold hurled herself from a high-dive platform into a sparkling pool. Tennis was being played by matrons dressed in crisp whites. And from the winding drive, I saw glimpses, too, of green and manicured fairways being traversed by gold-colored golf carts whose roofs were fringed in white.

The cab pulled up to the imposing entrance lobby, where a tall and muscular black man, dressed in some absurd kind of English colonial military uniform, right down to the white pith helmet piped in gold braid, waved us to a stop. With military precision, he lifted my suitcase out of the trunk, waved the cab on, and pointed the way to the registration desk. I wondered if he would call me "Bwana."

"*Sim salla bim*," I said as I handed him a couple of bucks.

"I beg your pardon?" he said. I noticed his gold-plated name tag said CARL. So much for colonial authenticity.

With Honie hovering about helpfully, I checked in. She had arranged a junior suite for me, which typically runs about $250 a day. The desk clerk passed over the registration form

15

to sign. I noted that in the place headed "Room Rate," it said "Complimentary. $0.00." All hail the power of the press.

We were assigned a bellman and went back outside to collect my bag. Just as we reached the curb, a gigantic black vehicle pulled in. Do they make stretch Bentleys? This thing looked like a mutant London cab: black, rolling fenders, some kind of enormous sterling hood ornament, oversized whitewalls, glistening grillwork, and tinted-glass windows. It looked to be at least twenty-five feet long.

I felt Honie come to attention beside me. Carl leaped to open the rear door of the black monster and, in an extra flourish, extended his white-gloved hand inside to aid the passenger's disembarkation.

Out of the car came Wynnona Haybrook Stilwell. She was one of the LPGA's few instantly recognizable celebrities. Wyn Haybrook had been one of America's finest amateur players as a teen. Tall, big-boned, and rangy, she had carved an impressive path through the golf tournaments of her day. She played a power game that few other women possessed: booming drives, crisp irons, and slam-dunk putts. And it was as a youth that she got tagged with her nickname. It was the newspapers that created it. "Another Big Wyn for Haybrook." "Big Wyn Does It Again." "Ladies' Open: A Big Wyn in a Rout."

As a pro, Big Wyn kept on *wyn*ning, both as Haybrook and then as Mrs. Stilwell. She became one of the Big Three in women's golf: Kathy Whitworth, JoAnne Carner, and Big Wyn. The distaff version of Palmer vs. Nicklaus vs. Player.

While, as with the other two, her heyday had largely passed, she was still considered a dangerous golfer—always capable of throwing up a low number on any given day. But Big Wyn continued to dominate the ladies' Tour in other ways. For more than ten years, she had been president of the Tour's Players' Association, and was a force in determining how the Tour operated. "Got to look after my girls," she was always quoted as saying.

Big Wyn Stilwell looked more the Queen Mother than a den mother as she emerged from the limo. She was still tall, but her

16

girth had increased some over the years. Still, she had an athletic build, with broad, powerful shoulders and strong-looking arms, and her skin was the deeply tanned shade of an outdoor person. Her golden brown hair was beginning to lighten to gray, and she wore it in a tight, short, manly cut, parted on the side.

Her face was the key to her celebrity: Its chiseled features were instantly recognizable. That defiant jut of jaw, those flashing, angry brown eyes, those strong-looking lips pursed in furious concentration. All that with the famous Big Wyn walk: tall, proud, arms swinging hard. It was a look that had been seen for years striding down the eighteenth fairway to the huzzahs of the multitudes. Even here, on a hot hotel sidewalk, one could look at Big Wyn and hear those cheers ringing in the breeze.

Big Wyn, once out of the monster limo, strode purposefully off into the hotel without waiting for the rest of her party. Climbing out after her was a small, pale man, balding above the temples, nattily dressed in a dark charcoal suit with tie and matching pocket square. Emerging into the bright Florida sun, he blinked rapidly against the light and clutched his brief-case tightly against his diminutive chest.

"That's Benton Bergmeister," Honie whispered to me, iden-tifying the commissioner of the LPGA Tour. Bergmeister caught sight of Big Wyn's stern disappearing into the hotel lobby and set out at a half-trot to catch up with her. I thought for a moment about the White Rabbit scurrying after the Queen of Hearts.

Last one out of the limo was one of those rare creatures—an honest-to-God, heart-in-the-throat, pulse-stopping head-turner. Long, long legs unfolded out of the door, followed by a torso that had been poured into a shimmering, ice-blue dress that just barely accomplished the business of clothing. And the package was topped as such a package should be: faultless blond hair, high cheekbones, sharp blue eyes, and pouty red lips.

She emerged as if in slow motion from the limo and stood there a minute, smoothing down that dress over a body that

17

should have been illegal. Carl flashed her a silly smile. I had the feeling that the world around us was reacting like one of those E.F. Hutton commercials. Birds stopped singing, insects halted their buzzing. The high diver froze in midleap and golfers stopped their downswings to stare.

I made some kind of strange, throaty groaning sound that came out something like, "Whozzat?"

Honie sighed the sigh of a woman who knows she's been licked and knows there's not a damn thing she can ever do about it. This package in the ice-blue dress was that good.

"That's Casey Carlyle," Honie said resignedly. "She's Big Wyn's, ummm, secretary."

I had to start breathing through my nose. My throat was suddenly inoperable.

Honie looked at me with no small measure of disgust. "Calm down, Hacker," she muttered. "You'll get to meet her in person tonight when you meet Big Wyn. I've got you scheduled for cocktails in Wyn's suite at seven. Casey'll be there."

"Eeeep," I managed to say.

"But I gotta warn you," she added, "Casey's reputed to be a real ball-breaker."

"Aaarrp," I squeaked.

Honie sighed deeply again, took my arm, and dragged me off to find my hotel room.

CHAPTER 4

H onie left me alone to kill the rest of the afternoon. I spent a leisurely hour or so wandering the grounds of the famed Doral, a place I visited every February when the PGA Tour arrived for the Doral Open, staged on the resort's Blue Monster course. A monster it is, too: long and winding and tightly guarded on all sides by trees and bunkers and water. It's a wonderful golf course, and a great test for the PGA pros, but it's not a place I'd choose to play just for the fun of it.

But Doral has four other courses, all bearing names of colors. The LPGA tourers would be competing on the gentler White course, east of the main hotel. And the hotel's guests were happily occupied golfing their balls on the Red, Black, and Silver courses. As at many resort hotels in this modern age of commerce, Doral's big bucks come from conventions and business meetings, not from Mom and Pop on vacation. As I wandered around, I saw the fleets of golf carts set up to handle the crush of business executives who would leave a seminar meeting room and head out to the course for a few hours of enforced sociability. One of Hacker's Rules of Golf, the firmest, is "Never play behind a businessperson's golf group." Instead, always head for the nearest bar. Because most of those who take part in such golf outings are, at best, twice-a-year golfers who hit the ball sideways with everything up to and including the putter.

Like most of the courses in Florida, the Doral's has a certain sameness: a terrain of monotonous flatness which comprises the greater part of Florida's topography. The state's golf-course architects have labored mightily over the years to break up that monotony by bulldozing the land into mounds and hills, digging out lots and lots of black, murky ponds, framing greens with stands of royal palms, and planting accent groupings of hibiscus and flowering myrtle.

But whether the fairways run straight or dogleg, despite the addition of ponds and bunkers and palm trees by the gross, golf architects cannot disguise the ultimate fact that the land is billiard-table flat, the sun is hot, and the mosquitos are fierce. That's golf in Florida.

Still, as I watched the garishly dressed tourists happily pounding away, I thought that this place was probably better than, say, a Chicago, no doubt still dressed in a coat of dirty winter slush, or a Detroit, a Buffalo, and or even a home-grown Boston on a nonwarm April day. Yes, for a day or two of golf, this place would do just fine.

I put such philosophical thoughts out of my head by thinking once again about that vision called Casey. Returning to my suite, I took a cold shower, turned on the sports channel, and promptly fell asleep.

I put a lot of thought into what to wear for my interview that evening with Casey . . . er, Big Wyn, of course. I thought about a nice Palm Beach pink linen jacket over some starched white ducks, with glistening Gucci white loafers. Sockless, for that extra touch of casual and studied nonchalance. But it was all thought. I am, after all, one of the mastodons of the press box, and we have certain standards of dress to maintain. Besides which, I don't own either a pink linen jacket or a pair of Gucci loafers.

So, I ended up in my uniform. Wrinkled khaki trousers. A mostly clean white golf shirt with only one button missing, but what the hell, I never button them anyway. My six-year-old navy blue blazer, which is only a little frayed at cuffs and elbows. Comes from leaning on lots and lots of bars. And, of course, Bass loafers with no socks. Like I said, we writers have standards to maintain, and at least studied nonchalance was one.

Honie came and got me promptly at seven. I was trying to brush back my hair in an insouciant flip when she knocked. Honie perched on the end of my bed and watched my efforts with a bemused kind of grin.

"So," I said nonchalantly, trying to keep my voice level and deep, "tell me something about her." I meant Casey, of course, and Honie knew it. Looking at her in the mirror, I saw her sly smile as she watched me fuss with my hairbrush. I almost had that last lock of hair where I wanted it. Kind of the young Marlon Brando look. Absolutely devastating.

"Okay," Honie finally said. "For starters, she sleeps with girls."

I dropped my hairbrush. Stared at Honie to see if she was pulling my chain. She wasn't. She was laughing her fool head off. I started muttering imprecations. No, what I did was utter some rather coarse oaths.

"Tell me, Honie, that there is a God and that this is not true," I pleaded.

"Sorry, Hacker," Honie said, wiping her eyes and going off into a fresh bout of laughter. "Signed, sealed, and delivered. There are lots of poorly kept secrets in this place and that's one of the worst."

"But, who? Why?" I was speechless. The waste, the utter waste of it all.

"I'll give you all the soap-opera stuff later," Honie said, glancing at her watch. "We've got to get over to Big Wyn's suite. She has been known to get pissed if you're late."

She stood up, then came over and gave me a peck on the cheek, sisterly like. "I'm sorry to burst your bubble, but I didn't want you to make a complete ass of yourself, at least on your first night here."

"Thanks a bunch," I grumbled, and we left.

I had thought my junior suite was pretty nice until I saw the penthouse palace occupied by Big Wyn and her party. Honie used a special key to send us in the elevator up to the top floor of the main hotel building. The elevator doors opened to an antechamber done in smoked mirrors and brass-and-crystal chandeliers. We walked down a curved hallway toward the sounds of low conversation and tinkling glasses.

We came out on the balcony level of Big Wyn's immense suite. The room that lay before us was semicircular, with two-story floor-to-ceiling window walls overlooking the golf courses. Beyond lay the twinkling lights of Miami at night. The decor of the room was Floridian elegance—white leather furniture, bright pastels on walls and accessories—all just a hint garish. The grand piano was white, lid propped open. A six-foot-tall flower arrangement featured lots of red, corkscrewed things.

As we stood there taking all this in, the conversation of the people standing around below us gradually stopped. I recognized Big Wyn, of course, who was wearing black evening pants and a loose white top. Benton Bergmeister, the LPGA commissioner, still wore his snappy gray suit and was clutching a tall highball glass. Standing over by the window, bedecked in a shimmering red-sequined floor-length dress, all luscious curves and secret shadows, was the lovely and unapproachable Casey Carlyle herself. I forced my eyes away after giving her a moralistic look of disapproval. She didn't seem to notice.

There were two others in the room I didn't know. A short, stocky, older man was wearing a crisp white overall getup, dress work clothes, that was unzipped down the front far enough so that wisps of grey chest hair peeped out. His face was full and deeply tanned, his receding hair almost totally white. He had powerful, sturdy arms and thick, beefy hands.

Standing next to Big Wyn was a thickset younger woman in a rather plain blue dress, which she kept nervously pulling and adjusting as if she were uncomfortable. She was not quite chunky, but solid and square in build. Her legs stuck out from the bottom of her dress like two strong fence posts, and I immediately guessed she was a golfer: They have that kind of power source. She had close-cropped black hair, a square, deeply tanned face, and an expression approaching a scowl. Her eyebrows were heavy and thick, which contributed to her overall unpleasant look.

There was a grand staircase before us that led down to the lower level where the rest of the party was, so Honie and I swept down. Honie handled the introductions with professional aplomb. I shook hands with Big Wyn and Bergmeister, whose grip was cold from holding his large drink. I noted that his cheekbones were faintly flushed.

The man in the coveralls was Harold Stilwell, Big Wyn's husband. The golfer was Julie Warren, who, it was explained to me, served on the players' committee with Big Wyn. Casey Carlyle smiled briefly at me from across the room when she was introduced, then turned and looked out uninterestedly into the dark. I believe I heard something of a snort from Honie, but I ignored it.

"Welcome, Mister Hacker," Big Wyn boomed at me in her deep subcontralto voice. "What can we get you to drink?"

"I'll have a Scotch rocks, thanks," I said.

"Harold, get the man's drink," Big Wyn ordered. "And I'll have another gin."

"Yes, dear," Harold said, and set off for the bar on the far side of the room.

"I'm still waiting for my white wine," Julie Warren piped up in a voice that whined a bit unpleasantly. Harold stopped and looked at her. He was about to say something but he caught himself and turned away back toward the bar.

"Why, I believe that I am about due for a refill," Benton Bergmeister said to no one in particular, and followed Harold. He lurched a bit as he walked, and I knew that he was at least two drinks ahead of the rest of us.

I noticed that no one had asked Honie what she wanted,

and was about to ask her myself when Big Wyn spoke up again.

"Thank you, Honie," she said, dismissively. "If we need anything else, we'll call your room."

A quick but discernible crestfallen expression crossed Honie's face when she realized she had been told to leave. She, too, had put some thought into her evening dress and makeup, and looked lovely. But she quickly recovered, gave me one of her 100-watt smiles, turned, and left the suite. I began to feel irritated. I'm not keen on authority figures anyway, but I especially hate it when they step so casually on the little people of the world. But what was I going to do, throw my drink in Big Wyn's face?

Harold came over with two drinks, mine and Big Wyn's. Julie sighed audibly. Big Wyn frowned at him. "Harold, will you please get Julie her wine?" she said imperiously. "She's waiting, y'know."

"Goddamn it, Wynnona," Stilwell exploded, "I only got two hands, for Christ sakes. You'd think a goddamn professional athlete would be able to fetch her own goddamn drink. I'm not a slave, y'know."

"That'll be enough, Harold," Big Wyn thundered back. "Get her drink and get it now."

I watched Harold's face turn a deep and dangerous shade of red. It stood out in sharp contrast to his stiff white coveralls. But the man swallowed hard, turned on his heel, and headed for the bar.

I took a stiff pull on my Scotch and wished it was my third.

"So, Mr. Hacker," Wyn purred sweetly, turning to me, domestic dispute behind her. "We are so glad to have you with us this week."

"Absholutely," Benton Bergmeister agreed, as he lurched back toward us from the bar. His shin struck the edge of a glass cocktail table and he stumbled, spilling some of his drink onto his hand and wrist. "Goddamn," he muttered. He recovered, stood up straight, and caught sight of Big Wyn's disapproving stare. He, too, turned red. He cast his eyes downward,

24

took a sip of his drink, and sat down hard on the leather couch.

"I trust your room is satisfactory," Big Wyn continued pleasantly. "If you need anything special, just give Casey a call. She is in charge of making the travel arrangements for the gals on tour, and she can make these hotel people jump."

"Well, I know *I'd* bust a gut doing whatever she asked," I said sweetly.

Casey turned back from staring at the window and fixed me with a totally emotionless stare. Her pale blue eyes just rested on me, unseeing. Flat. Dead. I got a bit of the willies looking at those eyes, and resisted the temptation to send a hand down between my legs to make sure everything was still there.

"And of course," Big Wyn continued, perhaps the hint of a smile playing on her lips, "Benton and I would be happy to make ourselves available for an interview at your convenience."

"Well, thanks," I graciously replied. "It's been a while since I last covered a women's event, and I'm looking forward to seeing some of the newer faces. Like Julie here, for instance." I nodded at the woman, who turned a little red. "How is your season going? I haven't heard too much about you."

Turning redder still, Julie was about to say something when Big Wyn cut her off.

"Julie has been working closely with me on Tour business so far this season. And as a result, her golf game has suffered some. But she has been working hard in the last few weeks, and we expect some rapid improvement shortly."

"I see," I said, as that little radar blip of irritation flared anew. I hate it when somebody answers another's question like that. "So what kinds of issues have you been dealing with?" I asked Julie, looking directly at her. "Have you found tournament sponsors to fill your spring break?"

The LPGA Tour had suffered the indignity of losing several tournament sponsors in a row a year or so ago, leaving a gaping, three-week hole in the Tour in April and May. So far, the Tour had been unsuccessful in filling this unwanted "spring break" in the tournament schedule.

25

This time, Julie Warren didn't even turn red. She just took a long, slow sip from her glass of wine, staring at me over the rim of her glass from beneath beetled eyebrows.

Big Wyn sighed once, audibly. "I don't know why that has become such a major issue with you press people," she said, irritation seeping into her voice. "Instead of focusing on the thirty-eight excellent tournaments we have scheduled, you always bring up those three damn weeks when we don't have one. I'll get those weeks filled, so just keep your pants on."

I turned to Big Wyn. "Well," I said, "since Julie apparently can't talk to me, perhaps you can point me at a few of the newer players who can. Perhaps there's one from the New England area? The local angle is always preferable."

For a minute, Big Wyn stared at me. An uncomfortable silence built in the room. "Of course," she finally said, and nodded, her eyes holding mine thoughtfully. "I'll be happy to give you a list of some of the girls you should talk to, some of our new players. Julie, you can probably help Mr. Hacker there, can't you?"

"Sure, Wyn, sure," Julie said, not looking too happy about the idea.

"That's very considerate of you," I said pleasantly. "But I'm kinda used to going my own way on things like this. I prefer to just poke around and get the lay of the place, if you know what I mean. Habits built up over the years and all that."

Big Wyn's eyes still peered into mine. I began to feel just a tad uncomfortable. Like a book being read.

"I understand, Mr. Hacker," Big Wyn said. "Still, I'm glad to have this opportunity to meet with you, and to go over some of our ground rules."

"Ground rules?" I inquired, trying unsuccessfully to keep the incredulity out of my voice. I put my drink down on the table.

"Certainly," Big Wyn said confidently. "Certain areas are, shall we say, not open for discussion with the girls."

There was such a sudden pounding in my ears that I felt sure everyone in the room could hear it. I glanced around quickly.

26

Harold was over by the wet bar, cleaning its surface with a wet rag. Bergmeister was staring into his drink. Julie was watching me with a hateful smirk on her face. And the Delicious Dyke was still over by the window wall. But she was watching us now, a slight smile playing about her lips. She held her drink glass in one hand, and with the other rubbed a sliver of lime around and around the edge. If I hadn't known better, I'd swear she was trying to do something erotic for my benefit.

"Such as?" I asked quietly, wanting to hear it all before I did something about that thud-thud-thud in my ears.

"Well," Big Wyn began, "first of all, I would like you not to dwell on off-course earnings by our leading money-winners. Everyone knows that the girls can make quite a bit extra through endorsements and advertising and such, but I feel it detracts from the image of the Tour as a whole. I prefer our girls to be known for what they earn playing tournament golf.

"Second, all figures on attendance at our tournament will come from our marketing office. We have very scientific and accurate data that will show the true numbers on our gate. Much better than the odd guesstimate.

"Third, the personal lives of our girls are off limits. We want you to write about their golf, and only about their golf. After all," and here she smirked nastily, "I don't recall reading anything recently about the private lives of the men players.

"Fourth—"

I stood up suddenly and held up my hand. I had gone beyond irritation, beyond that warning pulsing in my head. I was now, officially and absolutely, hot.

"Now wait just a goddamn minute," I said. "In the fifteen years I've been a professional reporter, I have never, until this very minute, ever been told by anyone how I'm to go about reporting and writing my story. For you to just stand there and check off your so-called ground rules as if you were reading a goddamn shopping list gives you the biggest set of balls I have ever seen in a woman. You can take those goddamn ground rules and shove them—"

"Mister Hacker," Big Wyn bellowed, as she jumped to her feet. "If I'm not mistaken, we have arranged for a complimentary hotel suite for you this weekend." Her cheekbones were burning. "And for some free meals and complimentary greens fees, if you want. I think that gives me some right to—"

"That gives you the right to stick it right up your wazoo," I retorted. "Do you actually think I can be bought for the price of a hotel room? Or a steak dinner? Jeezus Christ, Wyn, how many years've you been out here? What the hell are you driving at?"

"Casey!" Big Wyn whirled on the girl in the shimmering dress. "I want Hacker's comp cancelled immediately! If he wants to stay here, he can do it on his own nickel."

"My pleasure," Casey purred, and her dead, flat eyes came alive with a taunting, sneering gleam. She gracefully put her glass down and slunk off.

Wynnona Stilwell turned back to me.

"I want what I pay for," she said, staring at me through narrowed eyes. "And I get it, too."

I reached into my pocket and pulled out a five dollar bill. I threw it on the cocktail table. "That'll cover the Scotch," I said, "plus a tip for my waiter." I glanced over at Harold Stilwell, who was rocking on the balls of his feet, cracking the knuckles on his meaty right hand. He stared back at me.

"I'm heading for the front desk," I continued, "where I'm going to get the billing put back in my name. Then, I'm going to spend the rest of my time here digging into the personal lives of each and every player I meet, and I'm going to take a personal survey of their off-course earnings. And when I file my story, I'll be sure to mention the size of the gate this weekend. Oh, did I mention? I'm a really shitty crowd-counter."

"Why, you little fucker," cried Julie Warren. She slammed down her wine glass and started toward me with sheer mayhem in her eyes. Those thick, heavy eyebrows were knitted in anger. But Big Wyn put out a hand and stopped her.

"Take your best shot, Hacker," Big Wyn purred ominously. "Better men than you've tried and failed."

I couldn't think of a retort better than "So's your old man," so I turned and quickly left.

28

CHAPTER 5

Anger is a powerful human emotion. I reflected on that, but not for fifteen minutes or so. During that time, I was too busy seeing red. I don't remember storming out of Big Wyn's palace, riding the private elevator, stalking through the lobby, pushing out the doors, and wandering aimlessly out onto the golf course. I'm damn lucky I didn't fall into one of the Doral's lagoons and either drown or get eaten by an alligator.

When I came to, I was holding the black plastic knob of a ball washer in my hand. And my hand was throbbing a little. I looked around, momentarily befuddled. I realized I was standing on a tee somewhere out on one of the Doral Country Club's five golf courses. I had just trashed the ball washer, snapping its top off. Off in the distance, maybe a thousand yards away, I could see the bright lights of the main hotel building creating a halo of light in the humid mist of the Miami night.

That's when I began to reflect on the power of anger. Oh, everyone gets pissed, now and then. A cutting remark from the wife, a smartass crack from the kid, an insolent response from

29

an employee paid to know better. The blood pounds and the eyes narrow, and sharp and ugly retorts jump unbidden to the lips.

But anger, pure and deep, that's another matter altogether. I wondered, standing out there on the whatever tee, mosquitos and other carnivorous bugs zeroing in on my flesh, whether the first *Homo erecti* had ever utilized the emotion as part of their survival. They had hunted and killed the tiger and the mammoth out of instinct sharpened by several measures of raw fear, and driven by need and hunger. But there must have been times when the tiger had turned suddenly and dispatched the cave dweller's best friend or father or son. When the shock of that event had instantly dispelled all sense of fear and rationality and common sense in the face of pure, blind rage. And in that overwhelming, senseless moment, the moment of pure and unadulterated anger, the snarling, fearsome tiger had had no chance. No chance at all.

The tigers are gone, but the emotion remains. In these days of enlightened civilization, when the eyes go blank and red, a Saturday-night special suddenly puts an end to that bitchy-once-too-often spouse, a butcher knife is suddenly plunged into a drunken, abusive chest, or a child's arm bone is suddenly and irrevocably snapped in two.

I walked slowly back to the hotel, feeling a bit foolish. No tiger had devoured my best friend. Nothing so drastic had happened. No, my professionalism had been insulted, that's all. And I had lost it, surrendered to that awful passion. I had stood on the edge of that fearful abyss, peered over the side at the awful demons cavorting below, and had, for a moment, wanted more than anything to plunge headlong over the edge to join with them in their loathsome games.

I was in desperate need of alcoholic sustenance, a balm for a fevered soul. My feet followed the thump-thump-thump sound to the Doral's disco, a round, mirrored room with flashing lights, a long, curved bar, lots of tables and padded rails, and a small wooden dance floor. It was not a jam-packed night, but there were plenty of people about.

I made my way to the main part of the bar and saw Honie,

surrounded by a small group of women. She was nursing a drink which looked blue in the strange lights of the disco. She looked up and saw me.

"Hey, Hacker," she cried, waving me over. "You done already? How did it go?"

"Great," I muttered. "I made myself persona non grata before the first free drink."

"Aw, c'mon. It couldn't have been that bad," she insisted, grinning up at me. Then she saw my face. I handed her the knob from the ball washer and saw her eyes widen in amazement. I motioned to the barkeeper, ordered myself a tall Scotch, and told her the whole story. Halfway through, she began gnawing at a knuckle, her pretty eyes wide and round and serious.

My drink arrived just as I finished. "Sorry," I said, "I guess I kinda got mad."

She blew her breath out with a rush, looking at the broken knob in her hand. Then she grinned at me and shrugged. "Aw, fuck it, Hacker," she said. "I may not have a job in the morning, but what the hell. That's tomorrow's problem."

That got me started again. "Goddamn it, if they try to do anything to you, I'll slag her ass in every goddamn newspaper and magazine that knows how to spell the word golf," I said. "That goddamn, brass-balled bitch . . ."

"Whoa, Hacker." Honie's eyes were laughing. "I don't know what they'll do. I don't think anyone's talked back to Big Wyn for about the last fifteen years. She might be upstairs having a heart attack right now, for all I know. Listen, they don't know that you and I are old friends. And they really can't fire me for bringing press people in . . . that's my job, for goodness sakes. So forget it . . . c'mon, let's dance."

She grabbed my wrist and dragged me out on the dance floor. It was suddenly crowded out there. As one record effortlessly segued into the next, missing nary a bass-thumping beat, the lights went down, and only a rhythmic pulsing spotlight, flashing in time to the music, backlit the churning bodies on the dance floor.

Honie and I boogied. I'm no Fred Astaire, but I can keep

31

from looking like a doofus. Honie had all the effortless moves of youth. She was rhythmic and fluid and sexy and carefree. Which is how it should be when you're twenty-five and alive.

When the next song began the lights came up a bit, and I could see some of the other dancers crowded around us. As we whirled around, I picked out some familiar faces belonging to some of the professional golfers I knew or recognized. The crowd on the dance floor parted momentarily and I saw the shimmering red dress belonging to Casey Carlyle across the floor. Her back was facing me, and she was dancing elegantly, with reserved, economical movements to the wild jungle beat. At first, I could not see with whom she was dancing, only the fingertips of two hands grasping her around that lovely thin waist. Then, on cue, the couple moved slowly around, and I saw Julie Warren staring at Casey with adoring eyes as they danced.

Something lurched inside me, deep down inside. The two women continued to dance, oblivious to me or anyone else. I wondered for a moment about that lurch. Was it homophobia? Disgust? Titillation? I wasn't entirely sure. Like most reasonably aware people of the late twentieth century, I knew that homosexuality exists and is generally okay as the choice of consenting adults. I like to think that I am nonjudgmental and accepting. Some of my best friends . . . etc.

Perhaps it was the openness of the dancing couple that caused the lurch. Even those of us who profess to be open and accepting still prefer gay people to keep their preference hidden away from our eyes. Yet here were Casey and Julie dancing in the disco with stars in their eyes. Or maybe it was a tiny residue of macho that lives deep inside me. Casey was an attractive female person, I like attractive female persons, but seeing her dancing with another female person equals . . . a lurch.

I was thinking these thoughts as I continued to swing and sway on the dance floor. My eyes drifted back to Casey and Julie, who continued to turn as they danced. As they swung around, just a few feet from me, I locked eyes with Casey Carlyle. She noticed me and a mean little smile played at the corners of her lipsticked mouth. Her cool blue eyes held mine as with a sudden motion she pulled her stocky partner closer to her. The look she gave me was clear: What you want, you can't have.

Was that it? A sexual challenge? I sighed. The battle of the sexes is ongoing and constant, but it's a fight for which I can never muster much enthusiasm. Life is too short and too precious to waste arguing over lines drawn in the gendered dirt.

As I continued to look around the dance floor, I noticed several more all-female couples, many of them including at least one young woman who earned her living playing professional golf. I don't remember feeling a return of my lurch, but I'll bet my eyes widened as I recognized some of the players.

Honie must have followed my eyes across the floor, because she suddenly grabbed me again and pulled me back to the bar. Going up the steps, I stood back to let a former U.S. Woman's Open champion—she had been leading money-winner last year—pass by on the way to the dance floor. She was grinning happily and leading by the hand a petite young girl with lots and lots of poufed-out blond hair.

At the bar, I reclaimed my drink and drank most of it down. I needed it. Honie stood next to me, watching the dancing, still moving with the beat, eyes alive.

"Wasn't that—" I started, nodding at the dance floor.

"Yep," Honie said, swinging her hips.

"And who was that she is, ah, dancing with?"

"Her manager," Honie said, smiling at me impishly.

"Ahh," I said, taking another drink.

"We're a very close-knit group, Hacker," Honie said. "Lots of girls travel with their managers, business partners, cousins . . ."

"I didn't know Casey and Julie Warren were related," I said.

"Actually, I don't think they are," Honie said. Her face was motionless.

"I see." I thought about that for a minute, as I studied the women dancing on the small wooden floor below us. "How do you feel about that?" I asked.

Honie shrugged her shoulders as she surveyed the twirling mass of people below us. "Different strokes," she muttered, lifting her glass to her lips. She turned to look at me. "Happiness is a commodity that's in pretty short supply," she said. "I think you should grab on to it wherever you can find it."

"Sounds like you're a convert," I said, and immediately regretted it. It sounded peevish and judgmental.

Honie's eyes flared at me, briefly. Then she smiled.

"I've got a boyfriend in Chicago," she informed me. "Of course, in the few weeks I've been in this job, I have been hit on a few times."

"What?" I was indignant. "Who was it? I think that's outrageous . . ."

Honie held up her hand. "Whoa there, John Wayne," she said. "Be calm. It's nothing I can't handle. After all, as a woman, I've been hit on since I reached the age of puberty."

"Well," I muttered, "I still think you ought to report sexual harrassment to Big Wyn or somebody."

"How do you know it wasn't Big Wyn who hit on me?" she said, and laughed out loud at the look on my face.

I was stunned and speechless. There was nothing I could say that would come out halfway intelligent. So I threw a couple of bucks down on the bar, waved at my older-than-her-years friend, and went to bed.

CHAPTER 6

The next morning, I ate breakfast in the hotel coffee shop unmolested. No sign of a fire-breathing Big Wyn or any of her ilk. No sign of Honie, employed or not. Just a few dozen tourists from the North, each of whom seemed to be engaged in reading the prices from the menu out loud. "Two-fifteen for a side order of bacon, Willard! Two-fifteen! Dat's out-ray-gee-yus!"

Later, I wandered out to the practice tee to watch the women warming up for the day's practice round.

Like I said, I don't cover the women's Tour much, so I don't consider myself an expert on the women's game. But I had of course covered it from time to time, and it was at the Chrysler Cup, a mixed-sex event where teams made up of PGA and LPGA players competed in a best-ball tournament, that the differences between the golfing sexes had best been illustrated for me.

"It's the muscle groups that make the biggest difference," one of the male pros had explained to me, well out of hearing of sensitive female ears. "Women simply don't have the same kind of upper-body muscle mass that men do. In the golf swing, that means men can generate more clubhead speed, which is why they can hit it farther than women. These gals," by which of course he meant the professional women golfers, "get their butts into it when they hit the ball, which is why they can get the distance they can."

By that, he meant that women professionals knew how to use the big muscles of their thighs and legs to generate more power.

"But if you watch closely," my male friend had said, "you'll see that the girls hit the ball lower than men. That's because without the same kind of upper body strength, they use more of a sweeping action. Men combine clubhead speed with a descending blow—that gives the ball height. So your average woman golfer's hitting the ball on a lower trajectory, with less distance. That's a pretty damn deadly combination," my golfing source had said.

"Now these professional girls here know how to work the ball pretty well, mainly because they're practiced enough to learn how to overcome their built-in physical restrictions," he had continued. "But you take your average weekend woman player. Most of the holes, even the short par fours, she's hitting driver, three-wood just to get the ball up around the green. Can you imagine playing golf, hittin' three-woods into every green?"

"I'd give the game up," I had said.

"You and me both, son," the player had agreed. "Goddamn architects ought to give 'em a break, so they could play the same game as the rest of us. But that would mean really shortening up most holes, and then the goddamn women's libbers start screamin' bloody hell. 'Whaddya mean our course is only four thousand yards long? The men's course is seven thousand yards.' Can't win that one." He had shrugged, and gone back to launching high hard ones from the practice tee.

I had kept his theories in mind as I watched that weekend's tournament. And I had seen examples that seemed to prove his point. There was one time when one of the women pros was faced with a shot up and over a tall tree right in front of her. And, once over the tree, the shot had to carry a bunker fronting the green. She elected instead to try a hit a low screaming hook around the tree. She could have gone over the tree, but not with enough distance to carry the bunker. I knew that a male professional would have had no trouble with that shot at all, no trouble generating both power and height.

I wandered up and down the practice tee all morning, talking with some of the players, watching others. They were all working hard in the hot morning sun, doing the drudge work of professional golf. Honing swings, checking alignments, working on maintaining the angles, balance, developing a consistent tempo and rhythm. Those who had their swings working were cheerful and upbeat, whistling and joking as they worked. Those who had not been playing well were concentrating at their tasks, scowling at the ground, muttering after each swing. Dark circles of sweat colored their shirts under their arms and between their breasts. As the hot Florida sun rose in the morning sky, the word "glamour" was not one that could be applied to the activity going on here.

For the most part, the golfers worked alone, though occasionally one would consult with her caddy. The golfers worked methodically through their bags, which stood as silent sentinels behind the hitting area. Like most pros, the women players had huge, thick golf bags, the better to display the logos of the companies the pros represented. The men pros had sponsorships from club and ball manufacturers, auto companies, and stock brokerages. The women's endorsements, I noted, ran to dishwasher detergents, cosmetics, and soft drinks.

I also noted a large number of the women had unusual head covers on their wooden clubs: The prevailing taste seemed to run to pink, fuzzy dinosaur heads or cute little puppy dogs. Your typical PGA pro would probably rather play naked than have a cute little puppy-dog head cover in his bag.

The caddies who weren't offering swing advice to their players had gathered near the water keg at the far end of the tee. While predominantly male, there were a few lady loopers in the group. They were all deeply tanned, and mostly scruffy looking—the universal look of those who carry golf bags for a living. And they were doing what caddies usually do: exchanging information about good restaurants, can't-lose horses, rock concerts, all the while keeping an eye on their hard-working golfers, to see if they needed more practice balls, towels, or drinks of water. Caddies are firm participants in the service economy.

The only looper I knew in the group was an older guy named "Bunny"—I had no idea, as usual, what name appeared on his driver's license—who I recognized from his occasional stints on the PGA Tour, carrying for one obscure pro after another.

I approached him.

"Hey, Bunny," I greeted him. "Who's hot?"

He looked up at me, his smallish, deep-set piggy eyes widening in slight recognition.

"Everyone's talking about this young kid by the name of Meg Mallon," he said. "Got a game that makes 'em nervous, y'know? But me? . . . I'd put my money on the mick over there."

He nodded down the line of players. I turned and looked.

Patty Sheehan, one of the LPGA's established stars, was the one he indicated. I nodded at Bunny and wandered down the line.

Normally a right-handed player, Sheehan had flopped a wedge over upside down—so the top of the club faced down—and was hitting balls left-handed with it. Amazingly, she was hitting them all straight and true.

"Well, here's big news," I called out. "Sheehan converts to lefty. But y'know, I think they manufacture special clubs that work from that side."

She looked over at me, laughed merrily, and came over to shake hands. Patty has the right attitude toward the game: Whether she shoots sixty-eight or eighty, she's always cheerful, upbeat, wisecracking. To her, it's only a game; and that's no doubt why it's a game that pays off big-time for her.

"I do this to work on my impact skills," she explained as she returned to hitting balls with her left-handed upside-down club. "Makes you focus on the clubhead coming through. It's also a good way to get your hand-eye coordination working."

We talked about her season to date, and a swing change she was working on. She showed me the progress: Turning around to the right side, she pulled another iron out of her bag and struck a dozen beautiful shots, all of which landed within ten feet of her target. She had a classic, picture-perfect golf swing, full of fluid motion, perfect balance, and balletic grace.

She stopped work for a minute to get a drink of water from a cooler set up on the tee. Down at the far end of the practice area, an Asian woman was hitting golf balls, surrounded by a noisy gaggle of photographers, video cameramen, and a dozen other small, dark-haired, jabbering men. It was Misha Kuramoto, Japan's finest female player, and another perennial favorite on the LPGA Tour.

"God, how I feel for that girl," Patty mused as she stared down the practice tee. "They are with her always, dozens of them. Every day. It would drive me stark, raving mad."

Kuramoto was Japan's Goddess of Golf. Her success on the LPGA Tour had made her one of golf-crazy Japan's biggest celebrities. Which is why her every movement was chronicled by photographers, TV cameramen, and writers from the Japanese press. She was never alone. She moved in entourage, on the golf course and off. They probably went through her garbage so they could report back to Tokyo what the Great Misha was reading, eating, and throwing away.

"Every time she pulls back a club, the hopes and dreams of millions of Japanese ride on it," Patty said. "Can you imagine that?" She shuddered, and went back to her work in blissful isolation.

To those who have never played golf, and even to those for whom the sport is something less than an obsession, it might be hard to imagine enjoying spending a couple of hours in hot and humid air, watching the repetitive striking of golf balls to no apparent purpose. But I was thoroughly enjoying myself. I know enough about the golf swing to recognize those who can do it right, and on the practice tee that morning, there were several players who were doing it right. There are those who say the way to learn a good golf swing is to watch the women pros, not the men, and there is some truth in that. There aren't too many idiosyncratic swings on the LPGA: Most of them come out of Hogan's traditional mold. Certainly, one can learn a lot about timing and tempo watching the women play. Men may hit the ball harder, but women hit it with more grace.

It was fun to stand there and watch them work through their bags. To interrupt gently on occasion to talk about some of the finer points they were working on: a grip change here, a shoulder turn there, whether or not the club should be laid off, footwork, swing thoughts.

It was lunchtime before I knew it. And I didn't know it until Honie Carlton came and got me.

I was standing behind Betsy King, watching her smack three-woods heavenward with her easy, slow-paced, upright swing. Honie appeared at my side and grabbed my arm affectionately.

"Hey, Hacker," she said. "Hungry?"

"Well, kinda," I said. "But didn't I just have breakfast?" I looked down at my watch. Twelve-fifteen. "Jeezus," I exclaimed. "Tempus really fugited today."

Honie laughed. I like a girl who laughs at Latin jokes. Shows a certain amount of class.

"Hey," I said, remembering last night. "Are you still employed around here?"

"Yeah." Honie grinned. "I got called on the carpet, though. You are definitely on their shit list. From now on, any press I invite special coverage from I gotta have approved by the commissioner and Big Wyn. They patted me on the head and said all young people make mistakes. God, I almost puked." She tossed her head angrily.

"I woulda told 'em to go sit on a six-iron," I said.

"Yeah, well, you're you and I'm not," Honie said. "And I still got plans for the future here, y'know."

"I suppose," I said. "I guess I just have a lower puke threshold than you."

40

"C'mon. Let's get a bite," Honie said, and we began walking back toward the main hotel building. "You know, you've become something of a celebrity with some of the girls." She peeked up at me mischieviously.

"Oh, shit, have they been peeking at me in the shower? It happens to me all the time."

Honie laughed. I liked her laugh: merry and natural. There was not much pretense in this one.

"Well, the word got around, somehow"—she grinned at me—"that you told Big Wyn off last night. Something about having big balls for a woman?"

"I oughta wash your mouth out with soap," I said sternly. "Besides, why would that make me a hero? I thought everyone around here thinks Big Wyn hung the moon and the stars."

"Oh, not everybody," Honie said. "There is a certain vocal faction which obeys her every command, but most of the players, while they respect her achievements in the game, get a little tired of her imperious ways. I would say that Big Wyn might not win any popularity contests." Honie paused. "That is, if it was a secret ballot."

For lunch, we headed for the Grill Room, which overlooked the eighteenth hole of the famous Blue Monster course. There was a fountain at work in the middle of the lake that guards the front of that famous green. There was a long and groaning buffet set up against the rear wall, and the tables were set near the windows.

Benton Bergmeister swooped down on us like a hungry buzzard as soon as we entered the room. He must have been watching for us. Today he wore an impeccable double-breasted blue blazer with nicely pressed seersucker trousers. Instead of a tie, he wore a rakish scarf decorated in a garish paisley design of bright blues and reds. He was shod in black-and-white patent loafers with accents of shiny brass. What a dapper kind of guy. He also carried a low, wide glass containing something clear and on the rocks, with a military-tint olive floating happily among the ice cubes.

"Hacker, dear boy," he gushed. "And Miss Carlton. You must come have lunch with me."

41

"I dunno," I said. "I'm not in any personal danger, am I? You aren't planning to stab me repeatedly with your cocktail sword are you?"

"Ah ha ha ha," he forced out. "Not at all, not at all. I think we need to start over. Got off on a bit of the wrong foot last night. Please, help yourself to some lunch and come join me . . . my table's over there." He motioned casually toward a banquette in the far corner. "I'll just get another little libation." He set off one way, and we went through the line.

" 'Stab me with your cocktail sword'?" Honie inquired, giggling while we loaded up our plates.

"Okay, so I flunked Rejoinder 101. It's the best I can do if I don't have any preparation time."

"I thought it was pretty good," she told me.

There was a small salad plate in front of Bergmeister when we sat down, with nothing on it but a few crumbs. He had apparently elected to lunch liquid today. As we sat down, he was washing down a handful of pills with his drink.

"Uh-oh," I said, "LPGA commish is a secret druggie. Needs illicit highs to get through his workday."

Bergmeister chuckled.

"Not at all, not at all, Mr. Hacker," he said. "When you get to be my age, things begin to wear out. The medical profession, bless their evil hearts, stands ready to prescribe an entire pharmacopoeia to cure all the aches and pains . . . this for the heart, this for the blood pressure." He sighed. "It's hell getting old."

He started to put his pill bottle back in his pocket, then shook it and said to no one in particular, "I meant to have this refilled before I left home. I didn't think I'd run out quite so soon."

"Call Casey," Honie suggested. "She'll get it refilled for you."

I took a moment to study his face as he chatted idly with Honie about Tour business. The bushy gray hair was carefully combed back behind his ears. In fact everything about the man was careful and precise: his clothes, his hair, his bearing. But I could see the artificial shades of red across brow and cheek; the ever-so-slightly increasingly visible capillaries; the darkened hoods above the eye. My years of hanging around with Boston cops, those lovable, Irish, two-fisted drinkers of boilermakers—shots of Bushmill's washed down with foamy brews—had enabled me to study the faces of some truly prodigious drinkers. I knew the telltales, and I saw them even on the carefully presented face of Benton Bergmeister.

He turned to me and leveled his gray-green eyes at me earnestly.

"I feel I really must apologize for the unpleasantness of last evening," he murmured. "Mrs. Stilwell has been under a great deal of pressure in the last few weeks. She still maintains a busy schedule of tournament play because the fans want to see her. At the same time, her duties as president of the players' committee require a great deal of administrative energy. I believe she was just tired."

"Well, it's very nice of you to try and explain away her behavior," I said. "But she acted like a horse's ass. If she wants to tell me she's sorry herself, I can probably find it in my heart to forgive her. Everyone's allowed at least one mistake."

He took a long pull on his drink.

"Quite," he said, finally. "May I then tell Wynn that the hatchet is officially buried, and that we may expect a favorable article?"

I stared at him a minute, then turned and looked at Honie. She paused in midbite when she saw the look on my face. "Excuse me," she said quietly. "I just remembered something I need to take care of right away." She fled.

Bergmeister's question still hung unanswered over the table. He was idly stirring the ice cubes around in his glass with one finger, while he cocked his head at me, looking pleasantly as if he had just asked me if I would like one lump or two in my tea.

"You people are unreal," I said, slowly. "You never give up, do you?"

He colored. I'll give him that much. The man was embarrassed.

"Well—" he began.

43

"No. You listen to me, Benton," I said, still slowly and quietly. "I want you to understand my position here. I am a professional journalist. People do not tell me what to write or how to write it. If I happen to write something that you judge to be unpleasant or unfair or un-American, that's tough shit. You can write a letter to the editor and complain. If I happen to write something you judge to be libelous, you can sue me. And good goddamn luck.

"You see, I was planning to do kind of an overview piece here this weekend, something more than just a tournament results piece. Women's golf is booming in popularity, and theoretically the women's Tour is the vanguard of that popularity.

"But I find something more interesting here. You and I both know that the LPGA is struggling, losing sponsor and TV dollars to the men's Tour, and especially the senior men's Tour.

"And now a picture is beginning to form for me as to why that is. I see a goddamn pushy bitch is trying to run this business like it was a South American dictatorship, and seems to be doing a lousy job. And I see a commissioner who's not only her powerless front man, but a semi-alcoholic to boot.

"And suddenly, I got myself a whale of a story developing here. And when I come across a good juicy story like this, I do a little digging, and get a few sources to come across. And when I get through digging, I usually end up with enough facts to write the story. And that's what I'm gonna goddamn do. Got it? How 'bout another little pop? I'll buy."

I got up and left Bergmeister staring at me. He was slumped back in his chair, and his face had turned red, then white, then red again during my little quiet speech.

On my way out of the Grill Room, I happened to spy the lovely Julie Warren beetling her formidable eyebrows at me from a table near the door. My mood was just sour enough. I headed over.

"Hello, Julie, my love," I said sweetly to her. "Strangled any beagles with your bare hands today? Leapt any buildings

44

in a single bound? How 'bout castrated any sportswriters? I hear that's a big favorite with you."

She rose slowly out of her chair so that, standing, she was closer to being eyeball to eyeball.

"You're a lousy, good-for-nothing fucker," she said menacingly. "And I'm tellin' you, you better goddamn watch your back." Her forefinger was pointing at my chin by this time.

I grabbed her hand, pointy finger and all, raised it to my lips, and planted a noisy kiss on it, European-style. People at several tables turned to watch.

"God, I love it when you talk tough, m'dear," I said. "It gives me tingles all over." And I turned and left her standing there. I thought, "My rejoinders are getting better all the time."

CHAPTER 7

In the afternoon, I decided to trail around the golf course after Mary Beth Burke. She was playing a practice round with a young player I didn't know.

"Burkey" was a favorite of mine. And of a few million other fans. She came upon the LPGA scene a few years after Big Wyn had established her domination. Where Big Wyn played a rather stunning power game, Mary Beth had won our hearts for her pluckiness. Back in those days, she was like the girl next door: Small, tousled, freckled, she played the game with a ready, toothy grin and a "Never say die" attitude.

There had been several monumental last-day battles between the two players. Big Wyn slashing her furious drives, pounding irons into the greens. Mary Beth hanging tough, keeping the ball in play, draining those exciting no-brainers—long putts that no one expects to make—on the closing holes.

It had been legend-making golf on the order of Palmer vs. Nicklaus or Hogan vs. Snead, mainly because neither rival was viewed by the public as the bad guy. Big Wyn's style was power and dominance and was hugely admired by her fans.

Burkey was all heart: With her happy grin and her tousled hair peeping out from her visor and that inner determination to keep, by God, trying . . . well, you couldn't root against her, either.

Mary Beth Burke was a few years younger than Big Wyn, but her best golf was behind her, too. She still played a fairly active tournament schedule, I knew, but also spent a lot of time now teaching younger girls. I imagined she'd be good at that: never critical in a harsh way, always stressing the positive, and always planting the seeds of her indomitable desire to do better.

Her hair was still tousled, but it had gone a bit gray in places. Her grin was still there, and so were her freckles. I had interviewed Burkey several years ago at the U.S. Women's Open she had won, and had enjoyed the experience. I wondered if she would remember me.

I strolled out to the first tee as she and her playing partner were loosening up, waiting for the group ahead to clear the fairway. There were a just few fans about, so I was able to get right on the ropes, and caught Mary Beth's eye. ˙

"Hacker!" she exclaimed and came running over, that incandescent grin lighting up her famous face. "Oh, it's so good to see you again! I heard you were down here this week. What's it been, two years?"

I kissed her cheek and returned her hug gratefully. "I'm impressed, lady," I said. "It's been more like four. And it was only one interview out of probably a zillion you've given."

She leveled her sharp brown eyes at me. "I never forget a friend," she said. I believed her.

"Mind if I tag along?" I asked.

"Oh, that'd be great," she gushed. "As long as you promise not to write anything about my bad shots. And there are many of them these days!"

She waved to the other golfer on the tee. "Carol, c'mere. This is Peter Hacker, from Boston. He's a golf writer and a damn good one, too. Hacker, meet Carol Acorn. She's been workin' with me lately."

"Then she must be a damn good one, too," I said. Carol and

I shook hands. She was a rangy blonde whose straight hair was pulled back in a ponytail tucked back behind her golf visor. She had the broad shoulders and long, tanned arms of a golfer, and long, powerful legs. The crisp white shorts she wore accentuated her powerful thighs. Her eyes were a clear, no-nonsense blue.

"C'mon, Carol, hon," Burkey chirped. "Let's whack 'em!"

Mary Beth drove first, her short, powerful body coiling slowly, then releasing with a furious motion that sent the clubhead rocketing through the ball. The ball took off with the sound of resounding *smack,* straight down the fairway. The fans and I applauded, and we were rewarded with a patented Burkey grin and a soft wave of thanks.

Carol Acorn then stepped up to hit her drive. She stood behind the ball and focused those clear blue eyes down the fairway for a long moment before stepping up to the ball. Again, she paused at address for long moments, focusing on the task at hand. Her swing was technically correct, but there were slight and subtle hitches and twists and a discernible stiffness in the motion that made it seem unnatural. It was the golf swing of a robot, not a dancer. Programmed by computer, not inspired by a Muse. Uptight, not relaxed. Still, her result was fine, another high-arching drive down the right side of the fairway. She, too, was rewarded with applause.

Burkey motioned for me to come inside the ropes and walk with them. She looked at the handful of fans standing around the first tee and told them, "He's a writer. I'm in big trouble now!" They all laughed.

Between shots, we caught up on old times. Burkey told me she'd been divorced for a few years, but comfortably so. "Hell, poor ole Benny was in a lose-lose situation," she mused. "If he stayed back home in Texas, people'd talk about lettin' his woman roam the world without her man. If he came out on Tour with me, he became Mr. Mary Beth Burke. He spent a couple of years bein' miserable, until I finally told him it was time to do something else. It was like letting a man out of jail, Hacker," she said with a rueful grin. "We're still the best of friends, now that the pressure's off, and when I'm home in

48

Odessa we spend a lot of time together. And maybe in a couple of years when I retire for good we can try again. He's a fine man."

"And you're a hell of a woman," I told her. She rewarded me with another hug.

Maybe it was just the pressure-free environment of a Tuesday practice round, nothing on the line, not too many fans around. Maybe it was the attention she was paying to her student. Maybe it was the fun she was having talking golf and golfers with me. Anyway, I couldn't see much of a decline in Burkey's golfing skills that day. Without even trying, she was playing a plucky and brilliant game. Never a woman with great length off the tees, she kept the ball in play, fairway to green, and putted the lights out. On those few occasions when she ended up in a greenside bunker or sunk in the Doral's pernicious greenside rough, she slipped silently into her battler mode, and never failed to get the ball up and down with ease. Burkey could play the game.

On the tenth fairway, we stood together and watched Carol Acorn prepare her seven-iron approach to the green. Again, there was the deliberate planning and forethought, the long stand over the ball, the robotic motion of her swing. Again, the results were satisfactory, but not particularly noteworthy. The shot went on the green, about twenty-five feet from the pin.

"There's just a touch of stiffness in the swing, I think," I commented as we walked up to the green.

"You are absolutely A-One correct on that, Hacker," Mary Beth agreed. "The girl is a golfer. I knew that the minute I first laid eyes on her. But I'm having a god-awful time trying to get her to let go and just swing the club. You've noticed that she hasn't said word one to us."

It was true. While Mary Beth and I had been conversing actively between shots, joking and chuckling together, Carol Acorn had kept to herself, all business, her eyes hidden in the shadows of her visor. I couldn't even remember her speaking to her caddy.

Burkey laughed ruefully. "Once, on the practice tee, I asked

49

her what she was thinking before and during her swing. Y'know, we all usually have some kind of swing thought like, 'Smooth it,' or 'Slow back,' or something."

I murmured agreement.

"Well, this girl began rattling off all the things she was trying to think about while she swung the club. I mean, she listed not cupping the left wrist and maintaining the proper angles and feeling the clubhead open and pronating the left knee and on and on and on. After fifteen minutes of this stuff I almost took my driver out and smacked her with it. Good God Almighty, this game is hard enough without cluttering up your head with all that shit."

I laughed. "What was it that Bob Jones used to say? I think he said if he was thinking of three things before each swing, his game was in sad shape. If he only thought of two things before each swing, he'd probably shoot par. And if he only had one thought before each swing, he said he had a chance to win the tournament."

Burkey nodded her head emphatically in agreement. We got to the green. Carol's ball was away. She began stalking her putt. First she crouched behind it for a minute. Then she began walking all around the green, studying the angles, the break, the grain of the green. Then, back at the ball, she took about six practice strokes.

I heard Mary Beth audibly sigh. "Hey, Carol," she called out. We both looked over. Mary Beth cocked her head over, curled her fingers next to her ear as if she was grasping an imaginary drain plug, and pulled, making a loud popping noise as she did. She held the drain plug open for a long moment, cocking her eyebrows at her student as she did so.

Carol Acorn and I both laughed, and understood the pantomime. Empty your head, she was saying. This is only a goddamn practice round. Stop thinking about it and just do it.

Carol backed away for a moment, then, still smiling, stepped up to the ball, took a quick peek at the hole, and struck the putt. It rolled, with that uncanny, inerrant accuracy that well-struck putts have, right into the heart of the hole. Mary Beth shouted "Yeah!" and just grinned and grinned.

50

Carol loosened up measurably after that and began to sharpen her game. Her swing became smoother and easier, and her shots began to fall around the pins as if guided by radar. She even began to walk with an extra spring in her step, buoyant and confident. Mary Beth stood by watching, glowing with pride, always encouraging and praising the work of her young friend.

It was on the sixteenth hole that I accidentally crossed her wires. The sixteenth on the White course is a medium-length par-three hole, with a large pond fronting the green. The green sits well above the pond, partly contained by a stone wall that wraps about its front. There are bunkers all around the green, but well behind the green and all down the left side the greens-keeper had planted flowers, all in full and luscious blooms of yellow and red. The flowers soften the visual effect of the hole. It is a dangerous hole, requiring a well-struck iron to reach the small green and avoid the surrounding troubles. But those beautiful flowers all around and the reflection of the red stone wall in the still black pond attract the attention and deflect the concentration from the task at hand.

Carol Acorn had just made a lovely birdie on the par-five fifteenth, and I walked with her through a pine glade from the green to the tee of this beautiful hole.

"Gee, your game looks great, Carol," I said.

"Thanks, Mr. Hacker," she replied, a gay lilt in her voice. "Mary Beth is a wonderful teacher."

"How do you like the life of a professional?"

She blew out her breath in a whoosh.

"It's been a real experience," she said, shaking her head. "The level of play at the top is incredible. I've played in eight tournaments so far this year, and thought I played pretty well. Missed the cut in four and my top finish is thirteenth! But the other girls have been real nice . . . encouraging, y'know? And I've had a real good time."

"Have you ever played a round with Big Wyn Stilwell?" I asked.

She reacted to my question as if I had slapped her full across the face. She stopped cold and stared at me, her face draining of color, her eyes suddenly gone dark and cold.

"Wh-what did you say?" she quavered. "Wh-what do you mean by that?"

Mary Beth, who had been trailing us by a few steps, came up, and we both stared in amazement at the look on Carol's face.

"I mean, have you ever played with Big Wyn? You know, in a tournament?" I asked. "I just wondered if she's seen your swing."

"N-no," Carol said and abruptly walked on. Burkey cocked an eyebrow at me in silent wonder and hurried to catch up with her protégé. To give them a moment, I wandered over to a water cooler and filled a paper cup.

Carol had the honor (first shot at the next tee), due to her birdie. I could tell she was still upset. Her preshot routine was forgotten. She grabbed a club from her bag and took a practice swing with it—an angry, quick jab that hacked up a rather large divot. She did it again. And again.

"Hey, honey," Mary Beth cracked, "leave a little turf for the rest of us, okay?"

Carol did not respond. She teed her ball. Then, with a quick look at the hole, she stepped up to the ball and swung. Along with her composure, Carol Acorn had also totally lost her swing. Her backswing was rough and jerky, the clubhead well out of the plane. Without pausing at the top, she came rapidly down, trying to compensate for the bad backswing with a pull-through motion. On top of that, her hips got in the way and she ducked her head downward at the last moment.

It was an ugly, ugly swing with an ugly, ugly result. The clubhead was hooded, moving from outside to in, and it jammed into the turf. The ball flew in a sickly fashion to the right at about a forty-five-degree angle, carried fifty yards at most, and dropped into the pond with a soft and sickening plop. It was the worst shank swing of a twenty-eight handicapper, a twice-a-monther. It was the sort of golf shot that occurs almost daily at country clubs and municipal courses every-

52

where. But for a professional golfer, it was nothing less than shocking.

There were maybe six people standing around watching. I heard one sharp intake of breath. The two caddies stared at their feet. I didn't know what to say. Mary Beth Burke simply stared at her protégé, unbelieving. I know she wanted to say something funny to break the tension, but she seemed to understand that humor wouldn't work right here, right now. She was shocked into silence.

Carol Acorn held the pose of her finish and watched the ripples spread slowly out from the entry point of her ball. Those terrible, ever-widening circles stood as indelible proof of disaster. Then, she slowly lowered her club, walked silently over to a bench at the side of the tee, sank down on it, buried her face in her hands, and began, silently, to weep. Her broad shoulders shook.

Mary Beth hurried over, knelt down, and began to comfort the girl in soft, murmured tones. Carol seemed inconsolable. She couldn't seem to talk as wave after wave of some deeply buried sorrow came bursting forth. That it was all so silent made it even worse.

I was stunned. After a moment's hesitation, I followed Burkey to the girl's side.

"Carol," I began, "if I said something that upset you, I'm really sorry."

Her head came up out of her hands for just a moment. I saw the red, angry splotches on her face. And I saw her eyes. In that brief moment, I saw eyes reflecting unspeakable torment. Eyes from the Inferno. Eyes that revealed a terrible anguish and begged for relief from her private hell. But it was just for an instant, because she buried her face again, and turned away from me in misery, shoulders shaking again in silent sobs.

Mary Beth, who was plainly as perplexed as I, waved me away. There was nothing I could do. "I'll catch up with you later," I told Burkey softly and turned away.

I felt awful as I trudged back to the clubhouse. I wondered what had set the girl off so dramatically. Had the ugly brutality of that one bad shot been enough to send her over the edge?

53

Did she take the game that seriously? Had our small talk bothered her concentration? What was it we been talking about?

Big Wyn. I had mentioned the name and she had received a psychic jolt. Big Wyn Stilwell. There must be something there, hanging between the two. Big Wyn Stilwell and Carol Acorn. Something that could cause the gates of hell to open for the younger girl and let whatever demons existed come dancing out with their red-hot pitchforks and fiendish cackles and burning hot eyes and chase that girl's mind down and down into a region of boiling cauldrons and steaming, unrelenting heat.

CHAPTER 8

Mary Beth Burke came looking for me later that night, and found me in one of the hotel's bars. I was deep in conversation with a dentist from Pittsburgh. It was an intellectual discussion of batting averages, earned run averages, and slugging percentages of various members of our respective home teams. Inasmuch as I'm a golf writer and was deep into my fourth Scotch of the evening, I was proud of myself for holding my own in the conversation. I, of course, was defending to the death my beloved Sox, and the dentist for some reason seemed to feel the same way about the "Irates." From the looks we were getting from our fellow imbibers, we might have been just a decibel or two too loud.

Mary Beth Burke walked into the bar, saw me, and came over. She looked at me sadly for a second, then pulled me off my barstool.

"C'mon, let's take a walk," she said, pulling me out the door.

April in Florida is a pleasant time, about the last pleasant time until late November. The days are balmy without being overbearing, and at night the breeze drifts in off the water and brings with it just a hint of a cleansing chill. The worst of the blood-sucking summer bugs have yet to appear. I always figured the most carniverous bugs go south to Cuba for the winter and fly back across the Straits of Florida in time for the summer furnace of heat and humidity after having been made especially angry by a few months of life under Fidel's regime. Another few weeks, well into May, and day or night the air is a solid wall of humidity. Then, all the breeze does is move that humid air around slowly and ponderously, and force it up under your clothing to dark bodily places that begin to prickle and itch.

But as we strolled aimlessly through the softly lit hotel grounds, that whispering breeze was as caressing and refreshing as a sip of cold blush wine. It took some of the buzz out of my head. Mary Beth took care of the rest.

At first, she did a lot of fidgeting and sighing and mumbling as we walked together, her arm linked in mine. I let it sit for a time while I enjoyed the air. On the fourth sigh, I turned to her.

"Okay, Burkey, out with it," I said sternly. "What kind of burr you got under your saddle?"

"I need to talk with you—with someone—about Carol," she said. "But . . . I'm not so sure you're the one. You being press and all." She wouldn't look at me.

"Look, Mary Beth," I said. "I've got enough to write about without laying open some poor girl's personal problems. My readers don't give a shit about that. Now I don't know what set her off out there today, and I guess you're fixing to tell me. If it's something really deep and dark, don't tell me. Go find a priest or a shrink. If you think I can help with something, I'll listen. And I don't have to tell you it's all off the record."

She smiled at me again. "Thanks, Hacker," she said. "I think you'll do just fine."

We found a bench and sat down. In the relative quiet of the evening, the sounds of the city invaded the walls of our lush refuge. Off in the distance, a siren wailed. And a steady thun-

56

der built in intensity as a jet from the nearby airport roared its way down the runway.

"I didn't know what the hell happened to Carol out there today," Burkey began. "It scared the everlovin' shit out of me, to tell you the truth. She's such a steady, serious girl. Works real hard at her game, totally dedicated to getting better. Hell, if anything, I'd say she works too hard at it. But you know me, I'm more of the 'Let 'er fly and have some fun' school.

"But I had never, ever seen Carol exhibit any kind of emotion thing like today, on or off the golf course. I thought she was crackin' up. We had to come off the course, holed up in the locker room. Took me a couple hours to make any sense out of her."

"I mentioned Big Wyn Stilwell to her," I said. "That did it. I just don't know why."

"Well, you're sniffin' all around that dawg," Burkey said. "But do you remember what it was you said?"

"I just asked her if Big Wyn had ever seen her swing," I said.

"No, you asked her if she'd ever played a round with Big Wyn," Mary Beth said quietly.

"Yeah, that's right," I said. "So . . . ?" She didn't say anything. I thought for a minute.

"Wait a minute," I said, turning suddenly to look at Mary Beth. " 'Played a round. Played around.' You mean to tell me she thought I was asking if she'd ever . . ."

Burkey exhaled and nodded. I was speechless. "I know, I know," she said. "It sounds like a line from about a dozen bad jokes that you and I both know. But there's a bit more to it. And this is the real ugly part, Hacker."

She paused and looked out at the night. She chewed on her lower lip and clasped and unclasped her hands.

"Look, Hacker," she said finally. "You're a growed-up man, and you've been around. I guess it's no big news to you that there're some girls out here who like to fool around with other girls."

"Yeah, well, it's fairly common knowledge," I said. "Despite all the official tap-dancing about the subject, everyone seems to understand that for whatever reason a group of

57

professional female athletes seems to include a higher percentage of homosexuals than the population at large. So what? It's a free country."

"All true," Burkey agreed. "Most everybody agrees that what you do at night under the sheets and who you do it with is your own private business. From what I understand, that's been kinda the way of life on this Tour ever since there was a Tour. It's only lately that some people've been a bit more blatant about it all. Times change but still, it's something that's kept hidden from the outside world. The girls out here may have sex every which way, but most of them don't talk about it, or flaunt it in public. It's still kinda taboo."

She paused again, thinking for a minute.

"You gotta understand something about us, Hacker," she said. "The PR people like to tell folks that we're all one big happy family here on the LPGA Tour. I don't think that's quite the way it is. We're really more of a . . . a small town, if you think about it. I should know—I'm a small-town girl myself. There's about a hundred and fifty of us regular players, and our caddies, and our friends and family and business managers and whoever. And we're all kinda bound up together in what we do. When you think about it, that just about describes what a small town is. 'Cept instead of all being together in one place, like in Podunk, Iowa, we all travel around the country together."

"A movable Peyton Place," I said, suddenly understanding. "Same people, same life, different locale every week."

"Right." She nodded at me approvingly. "And like any small town, everybody knows everybody else's business, and then some. I get a wart on my butt, everybody knows all about it inside of a day. Then they all come over with butt-wart remedies."

I had to laugh.

"So what you're telling me is that Carol slept with Big Wyn, and everybody knew it," I said. "So why did she freak out?"

"No, that's not it at all," Burkey said. "Nobody knew nothing. Look, I told you how Carol is. She's got this one-track mind: golf, golf, and golf. I don't know what that girl

58

does just for fun, but I can just about guarantee that sex ain't it."

She paused again, her lips pursed.

"You see, we all know pretty much who does what and with who," she said. "When a girl first comes on tour, it's part of the list: she plays Taylor Made woods, Titleist 90 balls, and sleeps with girls or doesn't. And that last part is then about as important to us as the first: It's just part of what you are. I don't know anyone who's judgmental about the deal. We just try to go along and get along and play some golf."

She turned to look at me.

"What I'm saying is that even though we all know what's goin' on, we pretty much don't care. And the word on Carol was that she was one of the nonsex girls."

"Nonsex?" I asked.

"You know, just don't care about it one way or another," Mary Beth said. "Girls who are really serious about their golf just don't do it. Period. Too busy practicin' and playin' and all. Carol Acorn is one of them."

Mary Beth looked off at the lights twinkling across the fairway, and we listened to the cool breeze ruffling the fronds in the palm trees above us.

"When I'm working with a girl, I always try to get to know her a bit," she explained. "You know, after hours . . . let's go out and have a beer. Do some girl talk. I like to find out what makes 'em tick. Hell, people make out like professional golfers is magic somehow. We're just folks like everybody else.

"Anyway, this girl never opened up with me. Hell, most of the time she didn't even want to go out. Always had her guard up, never let anybody inside. The original and still the champeen Ice Maiden."

Burkey shook her head sadly. "Just no fun in that girl. It's so sad. But I see it all the time. These girls coming up are just so damned determined to win, no matter the cost. It gets their life outa whack, if you know what I mean. If you spend your entire life chasing a rainbow and don't get it, it leaves you feeling kinda empty."

"And Big Wyn?" I asked.

59

Mary Beth pursed her lips and paused before answering.

"Wynnona Stilwell is one of the best golfers who ever played the game," she said carefully. "But she is not a nice person. She has never let anything or anybody stand in the way of getting whatever it is she wants. And she wants it all."

"Such as . . ." I prompted.

"Well, hell, it's no secret that Wyn runs this show," Mary Beth said. "You know, all that woman has ever done in her life is play golf. She made it all the way to the top and stayed there a long time."

"And now?"

"And now her ability as a player is lessened. Hell, age does that to everybody. And we don't have a Senior Tour . . . yet!"

We laughed together.

"I think she got into the administration side of the game as a way to keep control, keep her hand in," Burkey continued. "She decided if she couldn't play her way to the top anymore, she'd just take over and run the joint."

"But the impression is that she's done a pretty good job," I said.

"Oh, hell, yes, she's done a wonderful job," Burkey agreed. "Purses are up, sponsors are happy, we're getting a little bit more TV coverage, but . . ." She trailed off.

"I remember there was some locker-room talk ten years ago when she got elected president of the players' committee about some people she had stepped on hard. And there're still whispers about how she manages to pull off some of the things she does. You know, we're all still independent cusses. So an issue comes up, everybody's got different opinions. Somebody says 'No way' about something goes into a meeting with her, comes out all smiles and says, 'Hey, this'll be great!' But you look at them casting their eyes nervous-like at Big Wyn and you wonder what was said in that room. Now, I'm beginning to understand," Burkey said, and blew out a deep and frustrated breath.

"Carol finally told me what happened. It was a year and a half ago. Carol was pretty new to the Tour and still struggling.

60

Wyn came up to her one day and offered to work with her on her swing. Wow! Big Wyn Stilwell coming to me!

"So they spent an afternoon on the practice tee. Then Big Wyn invites her back to the room to see some swing videos, study mechanics. Pours some wine. Two or three wines. Probably something in 'em. Carol wakes up in Wyn's bed. Wyn is doin' some things to her she just don't understand."

Mary Beth Burke's voice had started to shake.

"Carol is horrified. She jumps up of a sudden and starts to leave. Big Wyn laughs and pushes her down and starts in on the hard sell. Tells her that to win on the LPGA, a girl's gotta concentrate on golf and that there's no room for men in her life. Men are messes and trouble and heartbreakers. Tells her the good players have always known this, and that's why they stick to girls-only in the bed department. Uncomplicates things, she told her. When you simplify the sex life, you can concentrate on golf, she tells her."

"What a crock," I said.

"Yeah, well, like I said, she got the hard sell," Burkey told me. "And when Carol still balked, Big Wyn dropped the other shoe. Told her that the preceding little escapade was all on videotape. And Carol's got two choices. She can come back for more, and welcome to it. Or she can just bide her time until Wyn needs a favor from her, and then decide what's more important: doin' the favor or havin' the tape sent to her daddy or somesuch."

"Jesus Christ," I said, awed by the evil of it all.

"Yeah," Burkey agreed. "And pore ole Carol, the champeen Ice Maiden, locks all this up way deep down inside—all the memories and the guilt and the bad feelings—and keeps it there for a year and a half . . ."

"Until Hacker the scribe asks a simple and innocent, yet potent, question," I finished.

Burkey nodded sadly. "Whereupon it all came gushing out," she said.

"Where's the girl now?" I asked.

"I sent her home," Mary Beth said. "Withdrew her from the tournament, contacted her family, packed her up, and took

61

her to the plane. She's not in good shape. I told her brother to get her to a shrink and to do it fast."

We sat in silence for a long time, each locked into our own thoughts. It is always sobering to confront the evil that lurks within the human soul. It hides there within all of us, and most of us spend our entire lives working hard to keep it locked up tight. Oh, bits and pieces escape from time to time, surprising us and those around us with those short bursts of venality and hatred and badness. But most of us are successful in keeping it under control, bolted firmly down, hidden and secret and secure.

And then there are those who revel in it. Who let their personal evils come out and play every day. Who enjoy the power and the rush and the obliterating laugh of the daily fix. Who go through life happily destroying and tearing and burning.

Oh, it's no fabled battle between The Good and The Evil. None of us have the purity of heart and soul to do battle with the bad guys. We're all just trying to hang on, do the best we can, carve a little happiness out of whatever bad situation we're in. And then come The Evil Ones, catching us unaware from behind. Scything and slaying blindly. And as we fall, with our last conscious thoughts, we hear their victorious cackles echo in our minds.

CHAPTER 9

It was Wednesday morning when the telephone rang. Early Wednesday morning. Too damn early. I had planned to sleep in. It was, after all, my vacation, and I needed to catch up on some sleep. Especially since I had returned to the bar after hearing Mary Beth's tale, and gotten rip-roaring drunk. But the phone woke me a little after eight. After I discovered the time, I closed my eyes again.

"Morning, Hacker," chirruped Honie Carlton's obscenely cheerful voice. "Up and at 'em, big guy. A new day dawns."

"Ah, for cryin' out loud," I moaned. "Can't you just leave me be until after lunch? I promise I'll write nothing but lovely things about this goddamn Tour . . . just let me get some sleep."

I realized suddenly that my head was throbbing, my tongue was thick, and I felt, overall, like crap.

"I got a better idea," Honie said. "How about an entire whole day at the beach? Doing nothing but catching some rays, watching beach bunnies, and drinking piña coladas."

One of my eyes came open. "You are, as they say, playing my song," I said. "What's the catch?"

"Hacker, you are so cynical," Honie complained. "What makes you think there's a catch?"

"Honie, there is always a catch," I said. "Always."

"Well, today is just a practice round. The pro-am is tomorrow. But there *is* a little Chamber of Commerce deal over at the Fountainbleu at noon," Honie said.

I moaned and closed the one eye. My head began throbbing in a higher key.

"But," she quickly finished, "you really don't have to do anything. I just promised I'd have you there. As far as I'm concerned, you can stroll by on your way to the bar to get another piña colada, and you'll have been there. After all, I can't make you work, now can I?"

I laughed appreciatively. "Okay, you win," I said. "When and where?"

"I'll come get you in an hour." She giggled. "Bring your sun block."

I ordered breakfast from room service, had a quick shower, downed a few aspirin, and perused the morning paper I found just outside my door. The local sportswriters were waxing ecstatic over the women golfers preparing to play in their town. Somebody had done a big interview with Big Wyn Stilwell. A sidebar that went almost all the way down the page listed her career victories. The front of the sports section carried a four-color photo of Big Wyn. They had taken two pictures of her: one in golf clothing, holding her driver; one in a business suit, clasping a briefcase. The two photos had been doctored and spliced together so that Big Wyn was shown half in golf clothes, half in a business suit. "The Two Roles of Big Wyn," said the headline.

The copy was effusive in its praise of the job Stilwell was doing for the LPGA Tour. The sponsors she had helped sign on, the tournaments she had helped arrange backing for, the appearances she made week after week. Not a word about her being a vicious, power-hungry, manipulative bitch.

By the time Honie collected me, I had downed most of the pot of hot coffee, black, and was beginning to almost feel human again. She wore some khaki shorts and a white top that covered her bathing suit. And a big straw hat and dark glasses.

"Planning on working real hard today, huh?" I jested.

"Well, hell, I deserve it, the hours I've been putting in," she said. "Besides, my only assignment for the day is to entertain you. So when in Rome . . ."

Carl packed us into a taxi and we set off across the various causeways over to Miami Beach. Sun-and-fun capital of the world. Jackie Gleason and the June Taylor Dancers. Yachts bobbing in marina after marina. Glistening high rises overlooking the ocean, home to the new generation of glitterati.

The reality? Block after block of numbingly depressing motel units, all housing elderly people engaged in a race against time. Which would run out first . . . the money or the health? Days spent waking up, sipping prune juice, popping the colorful array of pills, wandering down to the corner to sit outside, trying to make the newspaper last the morning, studying the obits for the names of friends. When the money got tight, cutting back from beer to Coke, then from Coke to water. Meat to soup to cat food. Trying to cheer dying spouses and friends, and convince themselves, with spoken words like "better than New York!"

Florida is, after all, a land where people go to die. By the millions, they seem to believe that a few extra degrees of warmth, or the sight of a nice sunset on the ocean, will inspire them to live longer and prosper. It doesn't work, folks. It just gives this state's particular Grim Reaper more to choose from.

But that is the hidden part of Miami Beach, the blocks that lead up to the beach. On the shore line, all is wealth and riches and happiness bought and paid for. With interest. Doormen and security guards and delivered groceries and dinners out and days and nights at the club and money earning interest and kids and grandkids coming for visits. On the shore, life is still hope and the future. The black despair is kept inland, in those hot and humid cellblocks.

I could never be comfortable at a hotel like the Fountainbleu. I already dislike New York, and the Fountainbleu is simply

65

the worst attributes of New York moved to South Florida. It is loud and brassy and brusque and hurried and expensive. It is guys with lots of gold chains around their necks and white glossy loafers; and broads with black bouffant do's, ostentatious dangly bracelets, loud voices, and enormous bosoms crammed into hideous bathing attire. There is a lot of finger-snapping and rudeness and competitive one-upmanship going on at the Fountainbleu. No, not the place for me, thank you very much.

Honie led me through the cacophony of the lobby, through the back doors, and out to the pool. The Fountainbleu has an enormous swimming pool, one side of which is a fake stone grotto. There's a swim-up bar inside the cave, and you can climb some steps and swoop down a water slide off the top. Whoopee.

We went out to the beach. Honie arranged for a cabana, ordered two extra-large coladas, stripped down to bathing suit, and lathered up. I enjoyed watching. I parked my chair half under the shade of the cabana—no sense in overdoing right away, I told myself—stretched out comfortably, and prepared to get acquainted with the inside of my eyelids. The warm morning sun beat down on the broad beach, and a quiet surf lapped at the sand. The warmth, the sun, and the sound of the water, in conjunction with the overdose of Scotch the night before, made me feel deeply lethargic and listless.

"Okay, Hacker," Honie said when she was finished lathering and was comfortably stretched out on her chaise. "Give."

"Eh?" I murmured. I was watching a particularly interesting purple string-bikini number strolling down the surf line and thinking that even if I wanted to give chase, my body would refuse.

"What have you learned about our big happy family?" she asked. "Knowing you, you've probably tripped over some of the skeletons in our closet."

"Is this an official inquiry?" I asked.

"No, you shit." She frowned at me. "It's a question from a friend who wants to compare notes. Remember, I'm in mar-

66

keting, or will be one day. I want to know if our public image matches up at all with the reality of our product."

"Well," I mused, "I have discovered that Big Wyn Stilwell has developed some rather interesting management techniques."

"Delicately put," Honie agreed.

"Tell me," I said, "Does she sleep with every golfer on tour?"

"I can't answer that," Honie said. "My impression is, only with those she wants."

"Like Julie Warren?" I asked.

"Well, Julie is part of Wyn's inner circle," Honie said. "Some of the girls call them Wyn's Mafia. There are about six of them . . . some are on the players' committee, some aren't. Like I said, I don't know and really don't care how many of them go to bed with Wyn, but all of them are pretty loyal to her and will do anything she asks."

"Such as?"

"Oh, mostly innocent stuff, like making promotional appearances, taking a sponsor out for a round of golf, doing interviews, and things like that. Favors, errands, special tasks."

"And how does the beautiful Casey Carlyle fit into this chummy little picture?" I wondered.

"Her official title is travel secretary," Honie said. "Making arrangements to help everyone get to the next Tour stop and finding rooms and cars and airplane seats for those who need 'em. Unofficially, she is considered to be Wyn's eyes and ears and those players who aren't part of her Mafia don't trust her."

"A cold heart in that warm body?" I asked. "What a pity."

Honie just shook her head at me in disgust.

"Well," I said, "I'm not sure the public is aware of the degree of, er, control, Big Wyn exercises over the affairs of the LPGA."

"But it's also true that she has not received the proper credit for the things she's been able to accomplish," Honie noted. "Since she's been president, purses have gone up, the number of tournaments has increased, and in general the Tour is a lot stronger financially. The woman has uncanny business instincts, and she's been able to pull off some deals no one else has. I've got to give her a lot of credit for that. Benton Bergmeister, as you've discovered, is a zero from the word go. But we need a man to schmooze with the inner circle of sponsors and TV advertisers . . . that's still largely a man's world. As for Wyn . . . Okay, she can be a royal bitch and she's had to step on some toes. But that's what women often have to do to get ahead," she concluded.

"Oh, c'mon," I protested. "That's bullshit."

We were interrupted by a gaggle of photographers. They were calling out directions to a group of LPGA golfers who they were posing on the sand with the ocean as backdrop. About half were dressed in golf clothes. The others were in swimwear. The publicity juggernaut rolls on in Miami Beach.

Honie and I watched in silence for a moment as the photographers cried for "Just one more."

"Can you imagine a group of PGA golfers volunteering to spend two hours promoting their weekend tournament like this?" Honie asked me.

"No way," I said, almost involuntarily.

"Of course not," she continued forcefully. "They throw money at the men, beat down the doors to do things for them. But we have to hustle to sell our product. Now, you could say that it's not really fair . . . Women professional golfers play the sport just as well as men. But that's not the point. Women just have to work harder than men to get to the same point."

"I don't know—" I started to protest.

"Oh, c'mon," she said. "It's the same in any business. You hire a man, you automatically assume he can do the job. All you do is give him an office, a desk, and especially a secretary, and you leave him alone. You hire a woman, there's always a question whether she can cut it. There's always the unspoken need for a woman to prove she can do the job, over and over again."

"You're damn right!" agreed a voice behind us. I looked around. It was Mary Beth Burke, dressed in golf attire.

"Oh, shit," I moaned. "I'm outnumbered."

The gaggle of photographers, who had by now attracted a sizable crowd of onlookers ever hopeful for a glimpse at celebrity, had moved on, back toward the hotel. Burkey pulled off her visor, sank down at the end of my chaise, and mopped her brow.

"How'd you manage to escape the sideshow?" I asked.

"Years of practice," she said with a sigh. She looked at Honie. "You're the new PR girl, ain't you?" she asked. Honie nodded. "Sounds like we finally got one with a head on her shoulders," Burkey said. Honie beamed.

A Fountainbleu waitress came up and I ordered a drink for Mary Beth and another piña colada for myself. My first one had mysteriously disappeared in about three gulps. Honie, I noted disapprovingly, had taken perhaps two sips from hers.

"We were discussing various aspects of the weaker sex," I said innocently when the waitress had departed.

"You mean men?" Burkey asked slyly, winking at Honie. They laughed, compatriots together.

"Har de har har," I said snidely. "Okay, the theorem on the table is that in today's world, women have to work harder to get ahead."

"Amen," Honie said.

"But we have not addressed the question as to whether or not women are entirely suited to the fires of competition," I said.

"Oh, my God," Honie groaned. "What year is this? I thought we worked all this out generations ago. Jeezus, Hacker, get with the program."

"No, wait a minute," Burkey said, holding up a hand. "I want to hear this. Hacker is no pig. At least, I don't think he is. I've always felt he had a brain in there somewheres. Let's hear it, Hacker. But it better be good."

I paused for a minute, getting my thoughts together. I was winging it somewhat, and I wanted to pull together some of the things I had been thinking about.

"Okay," I said, "Here goes. We've proved beyond a shadow of a doubt that women are just as smart, just as capable, just as intelligent as men. They can do anything men can do, whether it's brain surgery or playing professional golf. Except, of course, they can't pee standing up."

The groan that erupted simultaneously from Honie and Mary Beth elicited curious stares from sun worshipers on both sides.

I laughed, and continued. "But I've got this theory that says being competitive cuts across the grain of womanhood and exacts something of a psychic price.

"Look, no matter how intelligent and sophisticated we think we are, deep down, we are still animals, and our behavior is still controlled by our basic instincts: the need for food and shelter and to reproduce the species. When *Homo* first became *sapiens,* a certain separation of function developed between men and women. Men, whose bodies developed in such a way as to support physical exertion, became the hunters. Their job was to deliver the food.

"Women, on the other hand, were assigned the task of birthin' the babies and keeping the home fires burning, literally speaking. If men hunted for the fuel for life, women nurtured life's growth."

I paused. Honie and Burkey were watching me with the eyes of hungry tigers waiting for their prey to move out of cover so they could pounce. But they still weren't sure in which direction I would jump.

"Okay," I continued. "Centuries go by, mankind evolves, gets intelligence, invents the wheel, learns agriculture and tool-making and the like, and the division of labors becomes somewhat blurred, except for the birthin' babies part. With the right tools, women can work in the fields, go hunting, run machines, take over the boardrooms, and play professional golf just about the same as men.

"However," I said, "I think that buried deep down inside the brain of every woman is a tiny little cell or two that keeps emitting a weak little signal. Kind of like a satellite way out in space somewhere, sending its signals back to Earth. And that little signal keeps saying, 'Nurture, nurture, nurture . . .' "

"So what you're saying is that we should all just be barefoot

70

and pregnant like God intended," Honie said angrily. "You sound like Phyllis Schlafly."

The waitress arrived with her tray of drinks. I passed one frosty glass over to Mary Beth and took the other. I restrained myself from offering to engage her in a chugalug contest. I was, after all, trying to impress them with my erudition at the moment.

"No, that's not what I'm saying," I contradicted Honie. "What I'm saying is that I really agree with what we were talking about before. Women have to work harder to succeed. Why? Because they have to overcome that tiny little primordial voice inside that's telling them they're not supposed to be out here slaying the saber-toothed tigers. That voice keeps telling them, 'It's not your job, honey.' "

They mulled on that for a minute. I did a little work on my new piña colada. My, it went down smooth, out there in the hot sunshine.

"Burkey," I said, wiping away a foamy mustache, "generally speaking, what's the weakest part of a professional woman's golf game?"

"The short game," she said quickly. "Chipping and putting."

"Exactly," I said. "And why is that?"

"Because they don't practice that part of the game as much," Honie said hotly. "Most women have to work so hard on getting distance with woods and iron, they just don't have time to spend practicing putting."

"Bullshit," I said. "Chipping and putting should be the best part of their game. Look, woods and long iron requires physical exertion, muscle strength, and power. Call that the male part of the game. The short game is all about feel and touch and a smooth and gentle stroke. Those are feminine words, if you will. Putting doesn't require a man's brute strength. It requires a woman's easy touch. So why can't women professionals putt as well as men?

"Because," I said, answering my own question, "it's where you close the deal. Y'know that saying, 'Drive for show, putt for dough'? The putting green is where you thrust that spear

71

into your opponent's heart, it's where you plug him between the eyes, push him off the cliff, run over him with the tank. For men, that kind of endgame is part of our psychic being. We have those tiny little satellite messages inside our heads, too. But ours say, 'Kill the son-of-a-bitch before he kills you.' So when a male golfer has to sink a twenty-footer to win, he can get the entire collective unconscious of the male species lined up and do it. A woman has this little nagging voice inside saying, 'Oh, dear, if you sink this putt, poor little Janie over there will feel real bad about losing, and you're supposed to make everybody feel good, not bad.' So she yanks the putt two feet wide."

There was a long moment of silence. The purple string bikini walked by and smiled at me. I smiled back, winningly.

"That is just about the most preposterous amalgamation of bullshit I have ever heard in my entire life," Mary Beth Burke finally said, looking at me levelly. I smiled at her, too.

"Okay, then try this one." I looked at both women. "Honie, both you and Burkey here have had a conversation with me in the last two days about the subject of lesbians in women's sports."

They both nodded slowly.

"Okay, so let's ask: Why are there apparently so many gay women in golf and tennis and other sports? The traditional answer is that playing sports is kind of a males-only activity so if a woman wants to play sports, she must be off somehow."

"But golf and tennis have always been acceptable sports for women to play," Honie protested again.

I nodded. "That's true, but when you talk about professional sports, you're not talking about country-club activities. You're talking about a serious profession, a vocation, and professional sports is not something women are supposed to do. Girls are supposed to be nice and quiet and attractive to men . . . They're not supposed to be able to rifle a two-iron into a guarded pin."

"I think you may have something there, Hacker," Mary Beth drawled. "Lord knows I took a lot o' shit from my friends and family growing up. My mom gave me dolls and tea

72

sets every birthday, but I just wanted to play with my dad's old set of clubs. Drove her plumb nuts!"

"Okay, so why do sports attract lesbians, or why are lesbians attracted to sports? My theory says it's because the successful female athlete has found a way to overcome that nagging little inner voice, and, in so doing, has become an unnatural woman. She ignores her natural inbred inclinations, that little nurturing voice, and learns to be different on the golf course or the tennis court or the swimming pool or wherever. She learns to become more malelike by adopting male attributes like being competitive, hungry, aggressive, a hunter. She represses and sublimates her female nurturing impulses."

I was rolling now. Mary Beth and Honie were engrossed, paying close attention. I took a healthy gulp from my drink and continued.

"And it's only logical to presume that sometimes this unnaturalness spills over into other aspects of her life, such as her sexuality," I said. "She becomes the sexual aggressor, the sexual predator as well, and seeks a soft, nurturing partner to fulfill her needs. It's simple."

I finished, pleased with my theories, and threw back the last of my piña colada. I saved the cherry, as usual, for last. The two women at first said nothing. Then they turned to one another.

"I think Hacker just called me a bull dyke," Mary Beth Burke said to Honie.

"I think I need another drink," Honie said to Mary Beth Burke. "Let's go get some lunch."

They didn't say anything to me. I figured I had 'em, blinded by my genius. Honie gathered up her beach things and we walked back toward the hotel. I was a few steps ahead as we passed the huge pool, feeling pretty proud of my reasoning abilities and philosophical understanding of womankind.

Until they each grabbed me by an arm and flung me, decisively, into the swimming pool. Proving yet again that there is nothing so dangerous as a hungry female tiger waiting to pounce on her unsuspecting prey.

73

CHAPTER 10

When we got back from the beach late that afternoon, there was an envelope stuck under my door. It was from the hotel manager, telling me politely that inasmuch as the Ladies' Professional Golf Tour had declined to honor the charges for my room, would I be so kind as to contact the front desk and make other arrangements. Screw you, too, I thought, and felt my stomach get sour.

I took a long shower and a longer nap. It was dark when I awoke. First thing I saw was that obsequious letter from the manager, and decided what I needed more than anything in the world was a drink. I dressed casually—no socks—and went down.

I stopped by the cashier's desk and let them take an imprint of my newspaper's credit card. I could feel a collective sigh of relief issue forth from the other side of the counter, although all I saw and heard were polite smiles. Loose ends make hoteliers very nervous, and until they have your credit card imprint on file in their hot little hands, you are a loose end.

I headed for the bar located off the lobby. It was getting late, and most of the other guests were already in having dinner. I felt like a liquid meal instead. Ordering a Scotch and soda, I cast my eye across the dark room. Half a dozen people talking quietly, heads close together. And off in the far corner, all by his lonesome, sat Benton Bergmeister.

He was on a bender. At first glance, you couldn't tell, but I'm an experienced bar-watcher, and I could see the signs. He was sitting too rigidly straight, for one. People drinking casually are relaxing. They lean on the bar or the table, cross their legs, and swing their feet. Their bodies are at ease.

Bergmeister looked as though he were sitting on the end of a long brass fireplace poker. His back was ramrod straight. His arms formed perfect ninety-degree angles, forearms placed symmetrically on the tabletop. His legs were also carefully placed under the table. Serious, experienced drunks frequently look like this. They try to give an appearance of relaxation and naturalness, but in their drunken states never realize they look wooden and contrived. It was one of the signs.

Bergmeister also had two glasses in front of him, another giveaway. One was virtually empty, just ice cubes and a lemon peel. The other was untouched and full. The waitress had probably tried to take the empty when she brought the new one, but he had stopped her, saying there was just one sip left.

People think drunks are sloppy, but the serious, professional ones are very precise. I knew that Bergmeister would carefully suck the last vestige of alcohol from the surface of each of those surviving ice cubes and then pour the ice melt into his new drink. Only when the glass was completely empty would he allow the waitress to remove it.

This operation also allowed the drinker more time between drinks, so that, again, he could present to the world the appearance of a drinker pacing himself carefully, not one slugging down drink after drink in a rapid fashion.

Because of my long years of experience with some of Boston's best alcoholics, I knew all these secret signs and signals. I knew, as I grabbed my drink and headed over, that when I sat down he would first be startled, then perplexed as he tried to recognize and place my face. Then he would be overly effusive in greeting to make up for that alcohol-induced momentary lapse.

Right again.

"Hi, Benton," I said loudly and suddenly as I sat down opposite him.

He jumped. Lurched, really, startled out of whatever reverie he had been in. He turned his rheumy eyes on me and stared for a long count. Who the fuck is this? Oh, yeah. Hinker. Holder. Hackley. No. Oh, yeah. The eyes widened in recognition at last.

"Hello, Hacker," he said thickly. "So nice to see you again. Have a drink?"

"Got one already," I said, holding my glass up for his inspection. He turned his eyes to look, then turned them back to me. "So what's new?"

"New?" he repeated dully. "New? Ah, Mr. Hacker, until today there was nothing new in my world. Just the old . . . as in same old bullshit. But, I am glad to say, there is about to be a whole vista of new in the life of Benton T. Bergmeister."

Wow. The old guy on juice was pretty eloquent. Too bad he was totally unintelligible.

"Well, that's great, Benton," I told him. "But what exactly are you saying?"

He took a good-size pull from his glass, the full one, then dumped the remaining contents of his empty one in. He glanced around the nearly empty bar and leaned over toward me conspiratorily.

"Can you keep a secret?" he asked in a stage whisper.

I leaned back and gave him my best winning smile.

"Secret is my middle name," I told him.

He straightened up and raised his bushy gray eyebrows in surprise.

"Is it now?" he said. " 'Secret' Hacker? That's a strange name."

He took another healthy dollop of booze and thought it all over. I could imagine his turgid, swollen brain cells trying to process the information, and all his imaginary amber brain-screen would give him back would be "Syntax error."

76

I waited while Bergmeister tried to think. Eventually, he gave up, and remembered his secret.

"I am resigning as commissioner of the Ladies' Perfeshional Golfing Tour," he finally announced, grandly and dramatically. He sat back and waited for my stunned and surprised reaction. I kept silent, instead, and after an uncomfortable pause, he finally looked at me with some disappointment. I guess he expected something different in a reaction.

"Finally got tired of the bullshit, huh?" I asked quietly.

It was like I had clicked the switch that released something inside the man. Even heavily boozed as he was, Bergmeister's bullshit tank emptied with a rush, and he spoke to me without pretense.

"Ain't that the truth," he gushed at me. "Ain't that the goddamn'dest truth? The crap I have had to put up with in this job was incredible. In-fuckin'-credible."

"How long have you been commissioner?" I asked, trying to remember.

"Seven and a half years, Hacker," he said somewhat sadly. "Seven and one-half long and trying years. I still don't know why they selected me. I was with the network in sales, you know, and was looking forward to retiring in four years. I guess Wynnona figured I could help obtain a better TV deal."

"Did you?" I asked.

"It's okay, could be better." Bergmeister shrugged. "But I had very little to do with it. Wynnona Stilwell was the one who worked on it. Woman negotiates with the best of them," he said. "Brass balls. Brass fuckin' balls."

"She must be hell on wheels to work for," I said.

"I have a bleeding peptic ulcer," Bergmeister told me, turning to look at me with pitiful eyes. "Every drink I take could be the one that kills me. Can I stop? Can I heal my innards? Not so long as that woman continues to rule my life. I am a nervous wreck. I can't sleep. I can't eat. I have had enough."

"Why'd you wait so long?" I wondered aloud.

"Hah!" Bergmeister snorted aloud. "That's what everyone says. 'Why don't you just quit, Benton?' 'Why don't you tell her off?' 'Just leave,' they say. Hah! You don't understand. You don't just work for that woman, she owns you."

"Nobody owns you, Benton," I said. "I think there's a constitutional amendment against it. You either let her push you around like that for all those years, or she's blackmailing you."

His back straightened. "I do not get pushed around," he said stoutly, with pain in his voice. He turned to me again, and his eyes had a painful appeal. I turned away and glanced out across the bar. I couldn't look in the man's eyes.

"I can see you don't believe me," he said, his voice dropping to a whisper. "Nobody would believe me. The woman is evil."

"Evil?" I echoed. "That's a pretty strong word, Benton."

"Not strong enough," he shook his head slowly. "The woman is a manipulator. It's not enough that she holds all the reins of power. She must control everything. No decision can be made without her approval. Any revenue source must include something for her. She doesn't manage the Tour, she dominates it. It's a need she has . . ."

His voice tailed off sadly. He stared into his glass, thoughts far, far away. Finally, he sat up with a jolt and took a large sip.

"What'd she have on you, Benton?" I asked quietly. If I hadn't heard Burkey's story of Big Wyn's vicious episode with young Carol, I never would have asked the question. But I was beginning to understand something about Big Wyn's management style.

"Wh-what do you mean?" he stammered.

His response told me I was on the right track. I zeroed in.

"Benton, you've been here more than seven years," I said. "Nobody with any dignity would take crap like that for that long. Like you said, you were ready to retire when you took this job. So it figures you stuck around because you had to. She had something on you. What was it?"

He took another long drink before answering, almost draining his glass. Instantly, the waitress appeared at our table, and Benton motioned affirmatively to her.

"I'll tell you," he said when the waitress had disappeared. He turned toward me with relief. His hands shook when he

78

raised his glass to his lips. I looked at him and saw his eyes had reddened with emotion. He seemed anxious to spill his guts to someone, anyone. It was more than the booze talking. Benton Bergmeister had a Lake Meade–size pool of anguish built up inside, walled in by his personal Hoover Dam. He had been waiting to punch a hole in that dam for a long time, and let the truth come gushing out through the thick, reinforced walls. He now felt that he could safely do this, and I was lucky, or unlucky, enough to be the one close at hand, the one to witness the lancing of his personal, internal boil.

"I'll tell you," he said again, and leaned toward me. "I've needed to tell someone for a long time."

"Is this off the record?" I interrupted. Normally, if a guy wants to spill his guts, you let him and figure out later what you can publish and what you can't. But I didn't want to take advantage of Benton's alcoholic state.

He thought a minute.

"Ah, fuck it," he said finally. "I don't care what you print about that bitch. She deserves anything she gets."

Benton Bergmeister took a fortifying swallow of his drink and got ready to tell me his sad tale.

Suddenly, there was a high-pitched scream from outside the bar, followed by a hysterical call for help. Bergmeister was glued to his chair by the effect of his nine or ten drinks, but I was among the first to jump up and run out to the hallway outside the entrance to the bar.

A well-dressed matron in a blue satin dress was standing there, her fist held to her shocked, open mouth. She was staring out the double glass doors that led to the outside courtyard.

Outside those doors, slumped in a heap on the sidewalk, was a young girl. There was a long, red smear of blood on the door, where Honie Carlton had pressed against the glass before sliding slowly down to the ground.

CHAPTER 11

I got to Honie first, while behind me I heard someone say, "Get an ambulance, fast."

She lay on her back on the sidewalk, her all-American face gray with shock and creased by rivulets of blood. Kneeling, I felt for a pulse on her neck. When I felt the steady beat, relief washed over me. She was hurt, but not in any immediate danger.

The blood was from a couple of nasty gashes on her temple and scalp, and I could see a bluish welling beginning to rise on her left cheekbone. Her eyes were closed, and when I gently lifted a lid, I could see her eyeballs had rolled backward into her head. That was not a good sign.

My examination was halted when I was unceremoniously jerked away by two extra-strong hands. They belonged to a heavy-set man dressed inconspicuously in khakis and a white short-sleeved oxford. The walkie-talkie affixed to his belt told me who he was: hotel security.

He made the same kind of cursory examination of Honie's inert body that I had just completed, pulled the handset from its leather clip, and spoke a few soft words into it. Almost simultaneously, I heard the soft bleating of a siren in the distant night air.

The security guy looked around at the small crowd of aghast guests that had gathered.

"It's okay, folks," he said calmly, holding Honie's head off the ground. "Help's on the way. Go on, now. Give us some room here. Thanks."

Slowly but obediently, the group turned and headed back into the bar. Standing at the doorway to the lounge, peering at us with her hand at her mouth in a pose of shock, was Casey Carlyle. I watched as she turned and sped down the hallway toward the lobby.

The security guy looked at me when I didn't move. "Husband?" he asked.

"Friend," I said. "She's with the LPGA group. Name's Honie Carlton."

"She staying here?" he asked. I nodded. He pulled his walkie-talkie and spoke quickly into it again. I could imagine the fast telephone call that would be made to the general manager. Hotel guest assaulted outside the main building. Possible liability. Get down here fast and begin damage control.

"Get lots of muggings around here?" I asked.

The security guy cocked an eye at me, but after a moment's pause, shook his head. "Very unusual," he said. "We'll close the place down tight, do a perimeter search. If there's a perp out there hiding"—he motioned toward the dark golf courses—"we'll get 'im." All the time we were talking, I noticed that he was carefully attending to Honie. He made sure her airways were unclogged and that she could breath. He held her head just above the hard concrete of the sidewalk, and he had pulled out a handkerchief and tried to get some of the blood off her face.

The siren whooped up to the hotel, and within a few minutes, two paramedics burst through the door. They took over from the security guy, made yet another quick examination, made radio contact with the hospital emergency room nearby, and sent for a stretcher. They moved with efficiency and skill. The security guy and I stood there and watched.

"Don Collier," the security guy said, holding out his hand. "I'm with the hotel."

I told him my name and we shook hands. "I'm going with her," I said. "She's an old friend." Collier nodded his assent.

The stretcher arrived along with three management-type guys from the hotel. Collier pulled them off into a corner and briefed them. He spoke a couple more times into his walkie-talkie.

Honie groaned once, softly, when they lifted her onto a stretcher. I grabbed her hand and squeezed. Then I followed the ambulance crew out to the driveway. I had to do some aggressive talking to get them to let me ride in the ambulance to the hospital, but they could look into my eyes and tell I was going with them.

On the ride to the hospital, the paramedic riding in the back with me phoned in to the emergency room.

"Mobile Three," he said into a radio telephone. "We've picked up the Doral call. White female, approximately twenty-five years old, contusions and apparent concussion, loss of blood, possible fractures to ribs, collarbone, upper arms. Over." He looked over at me. "They'll have a neurological workup ready and get the orthopedic surgeon on call down for a look-see. I don't think anything major's busted, but her breathing's a little wheezy, which could mean busted ribs. She'll be okay."

He looked down at her as we weaved through traffic.

"World's going to hell when they start attackin' guests at the Doral," he said a little sadly. "Druggies know where the money's at, though—all the rich tourists. Don't give a shit how it looks for the Chamber of Commerce."

He bent down over Honie and listened again to her breathing through his stethoscope.

Her eyelids flickered open briefly, and a soft moan escaped her swollen lips. I reached across the cramped aisle of the ambulance and grabbed her hand. It felt cold and limp and lifeless.

"Hey, kid, relax," I said, not knowing if she could hear. "We're on the way to get you an aspirin or something, so just hold on."

Her eyes came open again, and she turned her head to look at me as though through a thick and enveloping fog. "Murr," she said, trying to sit up. The paramedic and I gently pushed her back down. *"Murr,"* she said again, insistently. *"Wampy . . . herrninon . . . bulldosh . . . farrinch."* Her eyes closed again and she was silent the rest of the way.

At the hospital, I was politely but firmly held back when they wheeled Honie out of sight into the bowels of the emergency room. The paramedic who'd been driving took me to an orderly who took me to a nurse who took me to a small office where I was forced to spend a half hour answering questions posed by a bored clerk in front of a computer screen. I was not very good at answering the bureaucratic questions and when I began to wonder out loud if they were withholding medical services for a bunch of stupid questions and whether they were prepared for some major-league malpractice suits due to unnecessary delays, they finally let me go back to find her.

Inside, in a curtained-off section of a busy emergency room, a slightly harried doctor was able to reassure me that Honie was stabilized, okay, and would be held overnight for observation. Nothing broken, nothing damaged, pretty good concussion. All precautionary tests performed, results to be studied again in the morning. Patient medicated for pain and would sleep comfortably the night through. Come back in the morning, Mr. Hacker, sir, and she'll be able to hold a conversation. But not now.

So I taxied back to the Doral and went searching for Don Collier. The security office occupied a mobile trailer—a boxy, prefab structure well hidden behind the main hotel structure. Wooden stairs led up to the trailer's door, and a latticelike molding had been nailed into place around the base to disguise the concrete blocks on which the building rested. Going up the three stairs, I could feel the whole building shake.

Inside, Collier was alone, sitting at a cheap metal desk, talking on the telephone. The air inside was hot and stale and smelled of strong, burnt coffee. Behind the door I noticed a blackened glass globe coffee pot, with a half-inch of acidic brew curdling inside.

Collier's desk was military neat and mostly empty. The desk took up most of the width of the trailer. Behind it were a couple of beat-up file cabinets and a row of TV monitors, each showing a different view of some public area of the hotel. Red lights winked off and on below the monitors, on which the pictures changed periodically. Most of the views were of entrances and empty doors.

Collier hung up the telephone and looked up at me.

"Nice digs," I said.

He looked around and shrugged. "Not much sense making like Donald Trump," he said. "No one much comes in here except me and my men. All we do is keep it neat and clean."

I decided not to tell him about the coffee pot burning.

"Any further word on the mugging?" I asked.

He shook his head. "Negative," he said. "No witnesses as far as I can find, no sign of any nonlocals. We swept the golf courses and only found one couple engaged in nonauthorized activity on thirteen green of the Black course."

"Nonauthorized activity?" I asked.

Collier gave me a military grin, all eyebrows and half a mouth pulled up in a deathlike grimace.

"Let's just say we scared the pants back on 'em." He laughed. "These conventioneers can come up with the strangest places to make whoopee. Never figured out why they'd want to roll in pesticides and get their privates attacked by bugs when we have some of the most comfortable beds in the world. But, hey—" he shrugged—"it's their money."

The phone rang, and I watched the changing views of doors and entrances while he spoke briefly.

"I personally checked around that courtyard where Miss Carlton was assaulted," he said, after he had hung up. "Nothing there, but I'll want to take another look after sunrise. I did find Miss Carlton's stuff, though."

He turned to a little cabinet beside his desk and pulled a notebook binder and Honie's pocketbook out of the top

84

drawer. The binder was one of those bulky, daily-calendar efficiency things, with colored tabs and preprinted sheets designed to help workaday types organize every last facet of their lives. I have a deep and long-standing aversion to the damn things. I don't like to look at a blank page and worry about thinking of enough things to do to fill up an entire day. I don't like to preplan my day right down to the quarter hour. I prefer the freedom of deciding what to do next on the spur of the moment, depending on whatever I feel like doing next. I don't like feeling guilty if I can only think of two things to do for an entire day, and I don't like the feeling of seeing empty spaces on something that purports to represent my life. Besides, I've never seen one of the damn things that has a space on it for "Taking a leak." Guess that's not an efficient way to spend one's time.

"Mind if I take a look?" I asked Collier. He nodded his assent, so I picked up the notebook and began to leaf through it.

I found the section that had Honie's daily activities. She was obviously an organized person, but I decided not to hold that against her. Looking back through the last few days, I saw her scribbled notations, phone numbers and messages, and appointments for each day. Some of her entries were in some kind of personal code, and others had been crossed out, apparently when accomplished.

"Hacker A. 4:30 P.M., Flt. #478."

"Cocktails, 7:30, Wyn's suite. Send dress out for cleaning."

My heart sank at that one, as I remembered the pain of Honie's brusque dismissal.

I flipped to the page for today. Once back from the beach, her afternoon had been a busy one. She had babysat the local TV news crews and sportswriters doing some interviews, distributed a handful of publicity shots, checked on supplies for the press room, and called ahead to the next tournament stop, Sarasota, for some advance work.

There was a pencil notation at the bottom of the page that caught my eye. "Julie W., 5:30. Bring pub. cal."

"Did you see this?" I asked Collier, showing him the nota-

85

tion. "It looks like it was a last-minute addition. . . . Everything else on the page is written in ink, not pencil."

Collier nodded.

"Already checked it out," he said. "Julie W. is Julie Warren, one of the players. She's also on the players' committee, and she told me that she had asked Miss Carlton to discuss some future publicity plans for the next few tournaments. 'Pub. cal.' stands for publicity calendar. She said they met for about forty-five minutes in the Players' Lounge, then went their separate ways. Miss Carlton was assaulted about forty minutes later. Miss Warren went back to her room and took a shower."

I shrugged and went back to Honie's notebook. But I couldn't find anything that might indicate who or why. Still, I remembered, uneasily, Honie's description of Big Wyn's "Mafia," of which Julie Warren was apparently a member. Had Big Wyn sent Julie to beat up Honie Carlton? Even with what I knew about Big Wyn's management style, I couldn't believe it.

"Let me know if anything turns up," I told Collier. "Somebody whacked that girl pretty good, and I'd like to find out who."

"You and me both, pal," he said.

Walking back through the lobby on my way to my room, I was intercepted by Casey Carlyle.

"Oh, Hacker, there you are," she gushed, grabbing my arm. "I understand you went to the hospital with Honie. How is she? Is she hurt badly? Did she say who did this terrible thing?"

I looked for a moment into her cool blue eyes. Her words indicated a normal concern for a fellow employee. But her eyes were dead and flat, as they had been that night at Wyn's cocktail party. I got a sense that I was being pumped for information, more than seeing a genuine expression of concern. But I smiled at her and patted her shoulder reassuringly.

"Oh, she's banged up pretty bad, but the doctor says she'll

be fine," I said. "And nobody knows what happened yet. They'll try and talk to her in the morning."

"Oh, thank goodness," Casey exhaled. "I'll go and tell Wynnona."

She turned and took her beautiful self away in gliding steps, her long blond hair streaming behind her.

Call me a cynic, but as she went I wondered to myself if she was going to tell Big Wyn that Honie wasn't badly injured, or that Honie hadn't yet identified her assailant.

CHAPTER 12

I woke up very early the next morning, troubled and restless. I had been having a dream, one of those not-quite-nightmares, but strange and disturbing nonetheless. I had been in a conference room heavily appointed in mahogany panelling and brass fixtures, with gilded portraits on the walls. Sitting around the table with me had been Wynnona Stilwell, Mary Beth Burke, Benton Bergmeister, Carl the resplendently pith-helmeted doorman, Julie Warren, Carol Acorn, Casey the Delicious Dyke in an off-the-shoulder shimmering black dress, and I think Ronald Reagan, who was catnapping at the far end of the table.

We had been sitting around the conference table debating the real meaning of the words "Murr, wampy, herrninon, bulldosh, farrinch," which was what Honie had said in the ambulance the night before. The discussion, I remembered, had been quite heated. Reagan woke up at one point and tried to get a word in, but no one would let him speak.

Suddenly, the heavy double doors had swung open and Honie Carlton had walked in, wrapped head to toe in as much gauze as an Egyptian mummy. Though muffled by the bandages, her voice had sounded amused. "You are all being quite silly," she had said. "I said the damn words. The meaning is perfectly clear."

She was about to tell us when I woke up.

I got out of bed and stood for a long while at the window of my room, curtains pulled back so I could stare out at the soft, early-morning light that was just beginning to give some definition to the trunks of trees and the shapes of the oleander bushes. With the first hints of light came life, the first faint twitchings and stirrings of birds and insects and animals beginning their daily struggle for survival.

The early morning is melancholy, for me. Others feel the same about midnight, or the wee small hours. But for me, it's dawn. I could almost feel the cold damp fog begin to lick around my feet, working inexorably upward toward my heart and soul.

I don't know why. Daybreak is supposed to represent yet another victory over darkness and death, and should be a time to rejoice. But for me, it seems to be a reminder that the darkness is always there, lurking, waiting to return. We all spend so much time trying to keep that darkness away. But it's all just whistling past the boneyard. Because sooner or later, the scary and lurid places that dwell within take over. It's like those contrary symbols for the theater: the happy face and the death-mask grimace. We spend our days imagining our lives are a romantic comedy starring Rock Hudson and Doris Day when they're really the bleak and desolate landscape of *King Lear,* Act Three.

I shook myself, dropped the curtain, told myself to stop being so damn maudlin. Laid the melancholy to the events of the last few days . . . the conflict with Big Wyn . . . the squalid story of Carol Acorn's descent into hell . . . the brutal attack on my good friend.

Action. I dug out a worn and comfortable T-shirt, an old pair of shorts, and my beat-up sneakers. I am not a health freak nor do I aspire to ever be one. But sometimes I run. Jog, really, with lots of breaks for wind-gasping walking. I run not to boast to friends the numbers of miles I can do, nor to try and put myself in some kind of mythical fighting trim. No, I run when the spirit moves me, and it only does on infrequent occasions. Like when I look in the mirror and notice the old belly beginning to sag. Or when I have been a bad boy at the bar and need to sweat the devil alcohol out of my system. When I am bored. Or when I need to banish melancholy with physical action. If this exercise turns out to have some other beneficial side effects on my health, then fine, so be it. I could care less. In fact, every time I decide to run, I think about that guy who wrote all the running-is-healthy books who keeled over and died on a jog one day. I try not to do that. Drop dead, that is.

Of course, golf courses are pretty places to run through, early in the mornings before anyone is awake. As I started off down a fairway, the air was fresh and cool in the soft pink light of dawn. Dew hung heavily on the carpets of green, broken only by the tiny-footed tracks of some nocturnal animals who had scurried across the fairways before me. I ran down two holes, keeping to the cart paths and skirting the greens, until I worked my way through the painful beginnings of my run and settled into my second-wind, steady-progress pace. To get there, I run in cadence with my breathing: two steps per inhale, two steps per exhale. Once you hit that point, your mind is freed from the constant signals to cut this shit out and stop!

I held my steady, pain-free pace, admiring the world around me, beginning to awaken to the new day. Fat mullet flopped out and back in the ponds with loud splashes as I jogged past. Long-legged white egrets stood regally in the shallows, waiting patiently for a bold minnow to swim too close and become breakfast. The sun suddenly exploded over the line of wind-break pines to the east in a blazing ball of orange, and I felt a warm sweat break out on my arms and shoulders.

Ten minutes later, I was way out on the Doral property. I had lost track of which hole or even what color course I was on. I spied the figure of a man fishing in one of the murky lakes, and jogged in his direction. As I drew near, I made out the stocky figure of Harold Stilwell, dressed in denim coveralls and a fisherman's vest which was dotted with all manner of lures and flies. His tackle box was propped open at the base of a nearby palm tree, and Stilwell was casting his plug out into the lagoon with practiced flips of his thick and beefy wrists.

"Morning," I called out, panting just a bit. "Any luck?"

He grunted at me, staring at the water as he reeled in his line in short furious bursts, pausing between each burst to twitch the line between his fingers. I stopped to watch. Finally, he sighed and reeled his line up and out of the water.

"They're dickin' with me," he said, turning to me. "There's a big ole bass out here that I caught last year. I sent him back to grow. I know it's the same one, 'cause last year it was the same deal. He spent three days in a row nibblin' at it, spittin' it out, dickin' around with it. Fourth day, finally, the sucker hit it and I got 'im. I laughed in his fool face and sent him back."

He ran the hook end of his lure through one of the metal eyelets in his rod and reeled the line tight. He bent over and closed the lid of his tackle box, then stood up and looked at me.

"You're that Hacker feller, right?" he asked, looking me straight in the eye. I nodded. He looked thoughtful. "Gave Wynnona a big-time hissy fit. Had coffee yet?" I shook my head. He gave me a "Follow me" wave and turned.

I followed him around the lake and into a thicket of pines on the other side. In a shady clearing stood a huge motor home, sleek and powerful-looking. VISTACRUISER 98 it said on the outside. The machine was in its camping mode: foldaway steps pulled down, canvas awning extending over the door, aluminum table and folding chairs set up outside. I caught the scent of fresh-brewed coffee drifting out of the camper and through the clearing.

I laughed out loud.

"Wynnona Stilwell lives here?" I asked, unbelieving. "Campground for the stars? Don't the chiggers screw up her golf swing?"

Stilwell grunted. "Hell, no, you damn fool. She's got that fancy-ass hotel suite she stays in. Me, I can't sleep in those places. Don't like air conditioning and don't like a place where you can't open the damn windows. Naw, Wynnona stays up there. It's closer to the golf course anyway, and all that business stuff she's gotta do. Me, I like it better out here."

"Do you do this at every tournament?" I asked.

"Well, Wynnona makes sure they find me a good place," he said. "Some're better than others. Sometimes they just get me a place in the parkin' lots right next to Wyn's hotel, but then I begin to feel like a freak at the circus, everybody starin' at me. I like it better out in the open, where I can kick off my shoes. How do you take your coffee?"

I told him black and he disappeared inside the camper, returning shortly carrying two steaming mugs. The orange ball of sun had begun its work of the day, raising Miami's heat and humidity to near-unbearable levels. But here in Stilwell's glade, the shade of the trees retained a bit of the morning's cool comfort.

"Does Wyn ride with you between tournaments?" I asked.

"When she can, when she can," Stilwell said. "There's times when she just needs to get away from it all, so we crank this baby up and head for the nearest nowhere we can find. Do some fishing, listen to the crickets, admire the views . . . that kinda stuff. Helps her get her head back on straight, I think," he said.

"How long have you been married?"

"Oh, hell, more years than I care to remember," he said, laughing a bit. "I owned a nice little garage outside of Evanston, Indiana, and one fine summer's day here she comes, a smokin' and a coughin'. Like most women, she never bothered much with checkin' on a car's oil. Just kept pumping gas into her until she finally seized up.

"She was headed for a tournament, but in the time it took me to fix up her car, we got to talkin'." Stilwell paused and sipped his coffee, then stared down pensively into the blackness of his cup, as if he could see the events of that long-ago day, the bright cornflower blue of an Indiana summer sky appearing in its inky depths.

"She come back after her tournament, which she won, by

92

the way," he grinned over at me, a lopsided, happy, old man's grin. "One thing led to another and here we are."

"Sounds like a whirlwind romance," I said. "And it sounds like you give her something she needs."

He nodded at me, approvingly. "You're hundred percent on the money there, Hacker," he said. "I'm her backstopper. She's always been a house afire, never sits still, always something else to do. But from time to time she needs someone to listen to her bitchin' and moanin', or someone she can kick around and know it don't mean nothin', or just someone who tells her it's okay. That's my job."

He said this with just a hint of something deeper behind it. Pain? Anger? Heavy-heartedness? I almost held my tongue, but didn't.

"Do you like that job?" I asked.

He harrumphed and waved the question away with his hand as though swatting a swarm of mosquitos.

"She's a wonderful woman, deep-down," he said. "And it's been a wonderful life. Sure as hell better'n spending forty years cleaning the chinch bugs off the Widow Feeney's Chevy."

I sipped my coffee and thought for a moment. The insects in the surrounding trees began a buzzing song that ebbed and flowed in atonal melancholy.

"How much do you get involved in her LPGA stuff?" I asked.

"Not a whit and thanks to the Good Lord," he said vehemently. "All that jawin' and talkin' and meetin's and such is all her doin' and she's welcome to it. I'm a simple man, Hacker, and I'm gettin' to be an old man, and I treasure my peace and quiet."

"Somehow, I can't quite see being married to Big Wyn Stilwell and being able to find any peace and quiet," I joked.

He didn't laugh.

"What are you tryin' to say, pard?" he said with more than a hint of malice, staring at me across the clearing.

I held up my hand in peace.

"Nothing, Harold, nothing," I said quickly. "Just that what

I see of Big Wyn is a woman in constant motion, juggling seven things at once, and surrounded by a gaggle of people she's set in eight different directions at once. You know . . . Casey and Julie and Benton . . ."

He snorted derisively.

"Ass-kissers, every one," he said. "Bunch a damn ass-kissin' parasites, y'ask me. That Benton fella's pretty nice, though he takes more shit than a country outhouse."

He stirred in his chair and drained the last of his coffee cup.

"But I'll tell ya something, Hacker," he said, shaking a finger at me wisely. "I been out here with Wynnona for nearly twenty years now, and I seen 'em come and seen 'em go. And they all go sooner or later. Whenever they start lording their fancy asses over this lil ole country boy, I think about that. They might think like they're cock of the walk, but I know better. Sooner or later, they're history."

He was getting pretty wound up, and I was planning on waiting for more insight from Harold Stilwell. But just then, a dark green pickup truck pulled into the glade. The driver blew his horn in greeting and jumped out. Painted on the side of the truck were the words DORAL HOTEL AND CC. MAINTENANCE. The driver wore neat green coveralls and a broad-billed cap.

"Howdy, Hal!" he hollered. "Ready to tackle that mower engine?"

"Soon enough, soon enough," Stilwell muttered, and disappeared inside his camper again. He brought out another mug of coffee and introduced me to Charley Dillon.

"Charley's probably the best mechanic in South Florida," Stilwell told me.

"But I don't know half of what you already forgot about engines, Hal," Charley said, gulping down his coffee. He looked at me. "Man is a goddamn mechanical wizard."

"So you like to hang around the maintenance shed, eh?" I chided Stilwell. "Old mechanics never die?"

"Shit fire, man," Charley piped in. "I save up some tough stuff for when I know Hal's gonna be in town. With him around, I get my machines hummin'!"

I laughed and finished my coffee. Stilwell took our cups inside, closed up his camper, and climbed into the pickup with good ole Charley. I waved and headed back for the hotel at my slowest pace.

"Big Wyn and the Backstop." Sounded like a rock group. Relationships come in many varied shapes and colors, I know, but this one was strange. Harold was married to Big Wyn and Big Wyn was married to her job.

I couldn't help hearing that discordant tone in Harold Stilwell's voice as he described his "job." I wondered, and I wondered if he ever wondered, what Harold Stilwell got out of the equation. Wynnona got the freedom to pursue her career and the comfort of having someone to backstop her when times got tough. But who backstopped Harold? And how much backstopping could one man do with a woman as apparently manipulative as Wynnona Stilwell? Did Harold know about that part of his wife? Did he put his beefy arms around her and say, "There, there, Wyn, it's okay to step on people's toes and ruin their lives . . . it's okay"?

And what about Wyn's adventuresome sex life? How did Harold Stilwell relate to that? Did he know about it? Did he push it aside with his heated contention that it didn't matter because sooner or later they were history and he remained? Or did he just stay out in his homey little trailer and keep his eyes shut?

It seemed to me that the construction of the Stilwell marriage seemed to favor Big Wyn more than Harold. No surprise there. It seemed to me that every relationship that woman had favored her.

I began to understand why Harold Stilwell enjoyed camping out, away from the sound and the fury that must be a life with Wynnona Stilwell. Out here, there was peace and quiet, and probably loneliness . . . but there was also a measure of escape from some pretty harsh realities. I felt sorry for Harold Stilwell and admired the man at the same time. Not too many of us have the bullshit quotient of a Harold Stilwell. If he could deal with the weight of the circumstances of his peculiar life with Big Wyn and still find some measure of peace and satisfaction in it, that was admirable. I couldn't do it, and I don't know too many men who could.

Well, I thought, as I jogged slowly back toward the hotel, different strokes for different folks. Then I laughed at my own pun. Then I began to wonder when, if ever, the Stilwells engaged in strokes of a sexual manner. Then I began to picture Big Wyn naked.

That's when I decided I was suffering from oxygen deprivation or something even more serious and had better stop exercising and get something to eat, fast.

CHAPTER 13

After breakfast I cabbed back over to the hospital. Honie was sitting up in bed, holding an ice pack to her temples. Her eyes were darkly shadowed, and she didn't look like she was having a very good time.

"Hi, gorgeous," I said cheerfully. "Wanna dance?"

She looked at me with eyes of the damned.

"Fuck. Off." She enunciated each word clearly. "I want to die."

"Not feeling so hot, huh?"

"Everything I own hurts, plus a few parts I didn't know I had," she answered, and shifted her ice pack to the other temple. A nurse came in, checked her chart briefly, hovered briefly over the bed, and disappeared.

"Christ, there's a pro-am today and I had about seven zillion things to do," Honie moaned. "And I was supposed to set up some interviews for next week's tournament in Sarasota, and . . ."

"Whoa, girl," I soothed. "Relax, sit back . . . You aren't going anywhere. You almost got yourself killed last night, so

97

don't worry about bravely carrying on. Isn't there someone else who can do all that stuff?"

"Yeah," Honie admitted, shifting the ice pack on her head. "My boss, Karla, is flying in from Houston. I guess she can take over."

"Do you remember anything about last night?" I questioned. "Like maybe who it was who beat the tar out of you?"

Honie groaned. "Not you, too," she said. "That hotel guy and the police were in here at the crack of dawn asking me all kinds of questions six different ways."

"And?"

"I don't remember a thing," Honie said, looking at me, haunted. "I remember walking back toward the hotel and thinking how pretty that fountain looked in the pink twilight. Next thing I know, I wake up here with my head about to burst. Ah, shit."

She shifted position, wincing as she did. I reached over and squeezed her hand.

"What were you doing before it happened?" I asked.

She lay back and closed her eyes.

"I had been meeting with Julie Warren in the players' locker," she said in a soft and tired voice. "She was giving me a real hard time, so I was glad to finally get out of there."

"Hard time about what? Do you report to her?"

She cracked one eye open and looked at me through it, sadly.

"Like I told you, she's on the players' committee, one of Wyn's Mafia," Honie said. "So I guess I do have to report to her in a roundabout way. I mean, I report to Karla who reports to Benton who reports to Big Wyn and the players' committee. But it's like having the board of directors around all the time. All the players are equal, but the players' committee members are more equal than the others. You gotta suck up to them."

"So, what was the third degree about?" I asked.

"You," Honie sighed.

"Me?"

"Yeah. You know, how could I invite an asshole like you

98

down? What did I think I was doing? Didn't I know anything about you? What was I going to do to get rid of you? Christ, what a bitch!"

"What did you say?"

"I finally told her that my job was to get press coverage for the tournaments, and what the press chose to write about was their business, not mine. And I told her that I'd known you for several years and you were okay in my book. Then I packed up my stuff and left."

"So when you left, she was pissed?"

Honie opened both eyes and stared at me. "Well, yeah, probably," she said. "Frankly, I didn't notice. I'd been listening to her bullshit for half an hour, I had other things to do, so I just said my piece and left."

She looked at me funny for a minute. "But you don't think—"

Her thought as cut off by the arrival of the doctor, who greeted Honie cheerfully, then turned and asked me to leave. I went out and stood in the hallway, thinking. I remembered the sight of Julie Warren's red and angry face as she had threatened me in the lunch room two days before. Julie certainly looked big and strong, but could she have inflicted that much damage on Honie? More important, would she? What possible advantage could there be for Big Wyn that would cause her to order one of her own employees beaten? It didn't add up.

The doctor came out. "I've ordered another shot of Demerol," he told me. "She's still in a lot of pain, so I think we'll keep her here today. She's a pretty healthy young thing, so we should be able to let her out by tomorrow."

"Let me ask you something," I said.

"Shoot."

"Do you think she could have been beat up by a woman?"

"Only a very big or a very angry one," he said. "Funny you should ask, though."

"How's that?"

"The police asked me that same question two hours ago."

* * *

99

I got back to the Doral, went to the pressroom, and was told that Julie Warren, scheduled to play her pro-am round in about an hour, should be warming up out on the practice tee.

To get to the range, I had to walk around the front of the hotel, past that fountain that Honie had thought so pretty in the pink twilight just before someone had concussed her with gusto. There was no sign of violence on the pathway, just neat rows of yellow mums and red coleus, some trimmed box holly, and a palmetto or two for tropical effect.

Around to the side, the practice tee was busy. The women professionals were warming up side by side with their amateur partners for the day, who were busy trying to figure out how not to be embarrassed on the golf course today. There was a great deal of camaraderie, as most of the pros tried to help their partners find a semblence of a swing for the day's event.

The amateurs scheduled to play today were mostly male, mostly executive types from the tournament's main sponsoring corporations. Watching them flail away, I could see they were mostly twice-a-month players. They all seemed to have herky-jerky swings which resulted in lots of shanked shots or hard ground balls.

But the women pros were being helpful and encouraging, offering some hints and swing thoughts. Another difference between the men's and women's tours, I thought. While some of the PGA tourers are good with hackers, most can't abide pro-ams, and their arrogant attitudes show it.

I thought about my favorite pro-am story, featuring a gruff old pro from the Virginia mountains. As was his usual practice, this pro had, after initial introductions on the first tee, not only spoken nary a word to his partners, but totally ignored them. During the round, the pro so intimidated the four executives he was playing with that they spent a miserable round just trying to keep out of the pro's way, hurriedly putting out and moving on to the next hole.

Until the eighteenth. Walking up to the green, the pro had glanced at the scoreboard while one of the amateurs, reaching the par-five hole in regulation, quickly stroked his putt, leaving it about three feet short. Running up to the ball, the

100

amateur was about to pick it up, when the pro stopped him.

"Hold on, son," the pro growled. "If you make that putt, it'll be a net birdie and we'll finish in second place."

The amateur had stopped and looked at the pro, amazed that he had spoken.

"What do you mean?" the amateur had said.

"You get a stroke here," the pro had explained. "Your par will be a net bird and we'll finish in second."

"What's that mean?" the guy wanted to know.

"Y'all will get some prizes and I'll get about five hundred bucks," the pro drawled.

The amateur nodded. He marked his ball. Cleaned it carefully. Replaced it on the green. Took his time and studied the putt from three sides. Finally, he was ready. He walked up to the ball, took a couple of careful practice swings. Settled in over the ball, concentrating hard.

Then he looked up at the pro, gave him an evil smile, and whacked the ball clear off the green and into the lake beside the green.

"Fuck you," he told the pro, and walked away.

The stocky figure of Julie Warren was laboring in the next-to-last practice area on the long, wide tee. In the midday heat, dark patches of sweat colored her light blue shirt, causing it to stick to her skin. Her white visor held back her wet-looking mass of black hair. I noticed right away that she wore a golf glove on each hand. Interesting.

I went and stood directly behind her, standing behind a yellow rope strung about five yards behind the tee. She was punching low, hooking seven-irons at a flagstick in the distance. She didn't notice me standing there, so I ducked under the rope and walked closer. Nobody came yelling after me.

"Where'd you learn your boxing skills?" I finally asked.

She jumped a little, turning finally to see me standing right behind her. Recognizing me, she puffed out a sharp burst of air in reply, then turned back to her practice balls.

"I figure you must have lots of brothers, you're probably

00011

the youngest, so you grew up having to use your fists to defend yourself."

I might as well have been speaking to the air. Julie Warren ignored me.

"They probably taught you the basics, and I'll bet you used to be the playground bully, so you had lots of opportunities to practice. What I want to know is, do you like the feeling of punching someone's face in? The sound? The sight of blood? What is it?"

She turned to look at me this time.

"What the hell are you talking about, Hacker?" she asked, her eyes dark and foreboding.

"When you beat the shit out of Honie, did it give you a sexual thrill? Is that it? You like beating on people?" I began to get loud. There was a dangerous buzzing noise inside my head, and the fringe of my vision were beginning to cloud up. I was beginning to lose it. I sensed the golfers around us stopping their practice to look my way.

"You're crazy, Hacker," Julie said, although I could see her cast her eyes nervously toward the next practice area. "I had nothing to do with that, and you can't prove I did," she said defiantly.

"No, I don't suppose I can," I said. "But I'll bet if you take off those golf gloves, we could all see some bruised knuckles. It must be hell on the ole manicure to beat someone's face in. Those cheekbones can be so sharp."

I took a half-step toward her as the sky turned another darker shade of red and ugly. She raised her golf club menacingly above her head.

"You take one more step, shit-for-brains, and it'll be the last one," she growled.

We glared at each other. Why is it our society says it's not nice to hit a woman? They can be as hateful and ugly as men, sometimes worse. And this one, with her stocky shoulders, muscular arms, and thick upper legs, was no delicate flower of womanhood. Even if I could get the seven-iron out of her grasp before she planted it in my head, she would be tough to take. Especially if she was the one, as I suspected, who had

102

pounded Honie Carlton the night before. But I hesitated, for no other reason than it had been drilled into me since kindergarten that boys don't hit girls. I think she knew that, because she began to grin at me. It was an evil, you-can't-touch-me grin. It almost helped me overcome my deep-seated aversion to violence against a woman.

"Here, here," said a clipped, British voice behind us. I didn't take my eyes off Julie Warren and her raised golf club. It would be just her style to swing at my head when I wasn't looking. Women can be such dirty fighters in a clinch.

The voice stepped up into my view, coming between us. "I say, if you feel you must grapple, I will thank you to do it elsewhere," she said. "We are trying to accomplish some practice."

She was a fairly tall woman, dressed in a stylish navy golf skirt and red-and-white-striped polo shirt. Her reddish blond hair was pulled back in a ponytail, revealing a face that, while not pretty in the classic sense, was strong. She had wide shoulders and a trim athletic build.

"Julie, please put down that club and stop this nonsense at once," she said sternly to my opponent.

Julie obeyed. The woman then turned to me, her eyes angry and snapping.

"And you, sir. This area is reserved for players only. Spectators are limited to areas behind the yellow ropes. Kindly take yourself there."

I was finally able, once Julie's golf club was lowered, to look fully on our mediator. Her dark blue eyes gazed at me angrily.

"I'm Hacker, *Boston Journal*," I said to her. "Miss Warren and I were just discussing some alternative uses of a golf club. I believe Miss Warren intends to become a ecological big-game hunter when her days on Tour are over. Her ideas about clubbing the game into submission are much more sporting, don't you think?"

The eyes glittered anew, and the strong healthy face broke out in a toothy grin. From the throat erupted a strong and healthy laugh.

"Ha, ha!" she spat. "Jolly good! That's the spirit, eh, Julie?"

Julie apparently didn't agree. She turned on her heel, grabbed up her other clubs, and stalked off, throwing a last evil, hateful glance my way.

The laughter of my strong-faced friend followed her.

"Jolly good line, Hacker," she gasped. "I say, I fear we'll both be in for it now, though." She stuck out her hand. "Sybil," she introduced herself. "Sybil Montgomery."

I knew the name. Sybil Montgomery was one of Britain's better woman players, and part of a small, but growing, foreign contingent playing on the U.S. ladies' Tour. Unlike in the men's game, women's participation in the international golfing scene was not as widespread. The LPGA boasted a few good Japanese players, a tall blond Swede, one girl each from Spain and France, and Sybil and three other British players. There was a European tour for women players, as indeed for men, but Sybil and the others had decided they could earn more money playing in the USA.

"C'mon then," she said, grabbing my arm and pulling me off the practice tee, which had resumed its activity after our interruption. "It's lunchtime and I'm hungry. And thank God I don't have to play in the dreadful pro-am this week. You buy the lunch, Hacker."

What else could I do?

"Right-o," I said. "Off we go then."

She laughed again. I was beginning to like the sound of it.

CHAPTER 14

S o," I said, when we had gone through the buffet line, loaded up with chicken salad, a cold pasta, and sliced tomatoes, and ensconsed ourselves in a corner of the Grill Room, "What's your opinion of the Queen?"

"Needs more sex," Sybil said.

I choked on a sip of iced tea, and spent a minute coughing and laughing into my napkin. Sybil beamed at me. "Well, she does," she said, joining in my laughter. "Just look at her!"

I calmed down, finally.

"Besides," Sybil continued, looking across the table at me with narrowed and calculating eyes, "don't change the subject. I want to know why it is you wished to throttle the lovely Miss Warren a few minutes ago. God knows the creature deserves it."

"Would you believe a lover's spat?" I asked.

"Dear me, I don't think so," she replied. "Without the benefit of a peek inside your boxer shorts, I suspect you don't have the correct parts to appeal to that one."

"Ah," I said. Brilliant, witty repartee, that.

"So, you'll have to try again, Hacker," Sybil said. "I must warn you, the gossip about you is deliciously wicked."

"And what does all this yummy gossip say?" I wondered.

Sybil attacked her plate with gusto before answering. She gazed at me while she chewed, sizing me up. I did the same back to her. She could not be described as pretty, in the all-American sense of the word. Instead of the perfect cheerleader features, the pert nose, the perfect cheekbones, Sybil Montgomery had the classic English features: knobbly bones, a strong chin, slightly oversized nose, and deep-set, flashing eyes. Yet it all managed to come together in her to create a visually interesting and intriguing whole. She would never make it to the cover of *Vogue,* but her face was intelligent and interesting and alive. She looked at me with a frankness that was unusual.

"The gossip says that you have managed to alienate our führer," Sybil said, finally. "And it is known to be dangerous to clash wills with Big Wyn. The gossip further says that Big Wyn is trying to have you thrown the hell out of here."

"Well, even Big Wyn can't do that," I said. "There's still the First Amendment."

"But she can make life unpleasant," Sybil said. "And Julie Warren is often used for unpleasantness-making."

"Is she often used for physical abuse?"

"How's that?" Sybil asked. I told her about Honie's attack and hospitalization, and my suspicions about the identity of her assailant. Sybil's face darkened with concern and shock. "Dear me," she said. "That does go a bit beyond the pale."

I took a long drink from my glass and looked out the window, thrumming my fingers on the table.

"Look," I said, finally. "What the hell gives here? What's going on? What kind of operation does Wynnona Stilwell run, that she can just have somebody beat up and all you can say is it's beyond the pale? This is supposed to be an organization of professional golfers, not the goddamn Gestapo. I've never heard of anything like this."

Sybil reached over and patted my hand.

"Now, now, calm down, dear," she cooed. "You've got to

106

understand that Wynnona Stilwell is one of those people who wear power like a suit of clothes. It's what she lives for, and what she does best. She is a string-puller of the first order."

"But how?" I started. Sybil held up her hand to silence me.

"In all kinds of ways," she said. "She controls a lot of the sponsors' money, the how and why. That gives her weight. She is able to control which players get certain endorsement deals. Who gets nice hotel rooms and courtesy cars. Who gets interviewed by the media. If you're her friend, you get a lot of perks that make your life easier. If you're not, life on this tour can be an unholy grind."

"So everyone sells out for the money," I said sadly.

"No, not necessarily," Sybil said. "She has other ways of gaining the upper hand with some girls. Some not-so-nice ways, in fact."

I thought about the episode with Carol Acorn.

"You mean sexual," I said.

Sybil nodded. "Keeping your sexuality hidden is a major activity for many of the girls," she said. "The sponsors don't like to talk about it, unless you're married with children, in which case they feel it's okay to leer and make sexist remarks. The Tour would like to pretend all the players are either married or about to be . . . Hell, they even hired a beauty consultant to come on tour and give us all makeup lessons!"

I laughed. "I'll bet Julie Warren was first in line for that."

Sybil trilled her laughter, high and delicate.

"Anyway, that kind of heterosexual bias means that a whole lot of girls are running as fast as they can to get in the closet and stay there," Sybil continued. "It's sad, sometimes. I've known girls who tell their lovers not to follow them around the course because it might not look right. Can you imagine?"

She paused and looked out the windows at the green landscape.

"Wynnona Stilwell, I think, knows all about that, and knows which ones she can exploit," Sybil concluded. "And she does it without the slightest hesitation because of the power it gives her."

107

"But what about her husband, Harold?" I wondered.

"Perfect cover," Sybil said, laughing. "He spends most of his time fishing or working on engines, but he's an official husband who can be trotted out anytime Big Wyn needs the appearance of normalcy."

"She's sick," I said.

"Oh, absolutely." Sybil nodded as she munched on a carrot stick.

"So why do you put up with it? Why isn't someone raising the roof?"

"I don't have to put up with anything," she replied, staring at me across the table, coldly. "I play about fifteen weeks a year over here, win as much money as I can, and go back home to Europe to play. All my endorsement contracts and general fame and fortune are centered over there. Wynnona Stilwell not only can't touch me, she needs me, and the other European girls. We add class to her show. So she ignores me completely, except when she needs something from me, and then she asks politely. I expect, and get, nothing else. And that's fine with me. More than fine, if you really want to know."

"And the others? The young girls coming up who step into this and get run over?"

She let the question hang in the air for a moment, then looked away. I thought I saw something like guilt cross her face like a brief shadow, but I wasn't sure.

"It's not my problem, is it then?" she said, finally.

I said nothing. But a wave of sadness came over me. Sybil looked at me for a moment, then glanced at her watch, exclaimed over the lateness and her need to work on her putting, and left.

I don't know how long I sat there, staring out the window, lost in thought. But when I finally got up to go, the Grill Room was empty.

CHAPTER 15

W hen I was a boy, maybe five or six years old, some men from the city waterworks came to our street to do some work on the sewer lines that ran under the streets. I wandered out to watch, attracted by the big yellow truck with its flashing light, by the sawhorses set up a hundred feet on either side of the manhole warning motorists that work was in progress, and by the immense size of the truck driver—a ferocious, red-headed Irishman who looked positively Bunyonesque to me.

This Bunyon character, muscles bulging out of his stained white T-shirt, the sleeveless yoke kind, had grabbed a metal bar with a hook on the end, inserted it into the cast-iron manhole cover, and yanked it off the hole with a mighty grunt. It flipped over with a loud metallic clank onto the asphalt of the street. Suddenly, the street was alive with a dozen or more rapidly scurrying cockroaches—big, hairy, two-inch-long ones—awakened from a midday nap on their cozy and cool manhole lid and rudely thrust into the bright afternoon sun. It had seemed to me as though my muscle-bound friend had yanked the cover off the gates of hell, and these hideous black demons were scurrying around like crazy looking for lost souls to devour or tiny boys to cart back into the yawning black hole in the street.

I had run screaming back into my house while the city boys howled with laughter. The memory of that scene gave me nightmares for years.

It occurred to me that everything I had learned about the Ladies' Professional Golf Tour in the last seventy-two hours resembled closely that awful childhood afternoon. Almost against my will, the facade had been jerked back to reveal the scurrying, buggy rot underneath. I had long known that Big Wyn Stilwell had a reputation as a difficult woman . . . So what? And nobody in the golf industry was shocked anymore to learn that some women professional players were lesbians. Hell, there were undoubtedly some gay men players, too. So what?

The "so what" was that it was worse than that. Big Wyn was not just a difficult woman, she was a manipulative woman, and, it seemed, an evil one at that. Certainly, one who was not above using any tool, any means to add to her already significant power. One who seemed to be cruising through life, careless about the wrecked lives she was leaving behind in her wake. The emotionally trashed. The physically injured.

"Wait a minute," I said to myself. "So what? Why are you getting all hot and bothered? Like Sybil said, it's not really your problem, is it then? Who appointed Hacker the keeper of the universal flame of truth, justice, and the American way? Has anybody else jumped on the back of that noble white steed with its long, flowing mane and charged off into the fray to do battle? No. You're a goddamn golf writer, Hacker. You are paid to write pithy summaries of who won the golf tournament and why, and insightful sidebars on who might win the next one, and why. That's it, that's all. Nobody cares a damn about a shattered Carol Acorn. Nobody gives a shit about a concussed Honie Carlton. For that matter, nobody cares that Big Wyn Stilwell, one of America's most beloved sports heroines, is in fact an awful human being getting rich on the broken lives of others."

110

It was a great unspoken speech. But it didn't work. I cared. Was I just tilting at windmills? Probably. But dammit all, there are some windmills that need to be tilted at. And this was one of them.

I went back to my room and stood at the window for a long while, thinking, as I stared unseeing into the harsh light of the Florida afternoon. My reporter's instincts began to grind into action. "You have a lot of conjecture, rumor, innuendo, half-truths, and gossip here, buck-o," I told myself. "What you need are some hard facts and some corroboration."

I thought some more, playing things over in my head. Finally, I got what I was waiting for. That blessed "A-ha!" of an idea.

I went to the telephone and started to track down Danny Bell. Danny had been one of many old newspaper friends who had "gone on to bigger and better things." Truth is, working for newspapers is a never-get-rich proposition. You do it because you love to do it. Because you feel like you're doing something worthwhile. Because you just love getting out of bed in the morning and going to work. Because you love the cynics you work with. You love the pace of the work, and the feeling of accomplishment at the end of the day when you see your words in print. And because you love the game of it, the sticking of pins in the inflated balloons of our society, the revealing of secrets some would prefer be untold. And because you love the feeling of pride and power that comes from seeing the words you've created printed on a page in indelible black on white, the satisfaction of knowing that, in some small way, you are a part of a larger enterprise, something called the search for truth.

But you don't do it for the money, God knows. And not everybody can get past that part of it. Danny Bell loved being a newspaperman, but he wanted more. Needed more. There are thousands of people like Danny who do it for a while, have a ball, then "go on to better things." Higher-paying jobs, more responsibilities, the "real world."

Danny went to Detroit, got a triple raise when he went to work for an automobile maker. Public affairs or some damn thing. Wrote a little, attended lots of meetings, took people out to lunch, travelled some. Got paid big bucks for keeping his head down and out of trouble. Bigger and better things.

Still, I needed Danny. After passing through a few levels of secretaries and receptionists, I finally got him on the line.

"Hacker, my man!" he exclaimed. "How're they hangin'?"

"Fine, Danny, fine," I said. "Keepin' busy?"

"I've got a hellacious afternoon schedule," he said. "I got one telephone call to make and a memo to write. I tell you, it's tough to come up with creative ways to keep from falling dead-ass asleep after lunch in this job!"

I laughed and asked about his wife and kids. In Boston, the Bell family had crammed itself into a tiny two-bedroom Brookline flat. Now, they owned a spacious home in a nice Detroit suburb. Good schools for the kids, lots of friends and neighbors for the wife, probably belonged to a country club. The good life. Probably made it worthwhile, in Danny's mind, his having to abide all the bullshit. Probably.

"So to what can I attribute the pleasure of this call?" Danny finally asked.

"God, you're starting to sound like someone in public affairs," I chided him. "I need some background for a piece I'm doing on the LPGA," I told him. "I know your company used to be a major sponsor of the women's tournament up there. What do you know about it?"

He blew out his breath in a rush.

"The LPGA?" he mused. "Yeah, I remember something about that. I wasn't directly involved, you know. You'd probably get better information out of the marketing veep for that division. He was in the day-to-day trenches."

"Haven't got the time," I said. "Besides, I don't need total accuracy right now, just your general impressions. Deep background."

"Okay, sure," Danny said. "Let me think. We were tournament sponsor up here in Michigan for five years, I think. Research boys thought it was a good thing to put money into . . . said that most major purchasing decisions, such as buying a new automobile, were heavily influenced by females. And

112

that sponsoring a female sports event would attract upper-percentile attention. You know how they talk . . . impressions per million and shit like that. Demo-speak."

I made a gagging noise in my throat.

"Yeah, I agree," Danny said.

"I always thought that the men bought the cars," I said.

"I think they do," Danny agreed. "At least in terms of shopping, looking under the hoods, and stuff like that. But the stats show that women get heavily involved when it's time to make the final decisions regarding major household expenditures."

"So, did it work?" I wondered.

"Tournament sponsorship?" Danny asked, "Nah, not really. First of all, there wasn't TV coverage until the last year, and then only on cable. So our national exposure was limited drastically. Even you sports boys refused to use the full name of the tournament. It was always in the papers as 'the Detroit Ladies' Classic.' Didn't do us diddley-squat, you ask me. I think it was mostly an excuse for the prez to have a legitimate reason to sneak out and play some golf."

"So you didn't re-up the contract."

"Well, as I recall, there were some serious negotiations on renewal," Danny said. "And it seems to me that the reason we didn't renew was that the LPGA laid a whole series of heavy demands on us."

"Really? Like what?"

"Ummm, don't quote me, 'cause it's been a few years now. But I think they wanted a fleet of our top-line cars for the top Tour brass. And some major new bucks to become one of the entire Tour's sponsors. And . . . and this part is mostly rumor which came through the corporate grapevine . . . I heard something about an under-the-table demand for some appearance money for some of the bigger names."

"Jeez," I said. "Nobody gets appearance money in this country . . . only in Europe. It's downright un-American. Sounds like blackmail, almost."

"Yeah, something like that," Danny agreed. "The number I heard was a cool hundred grand, tax-free and silent. Our

113

legal beagles about shit their pants when they heard about it. IRS woulda chomped down so hard, everyone's dick woulda fallen off."

I laughed. "Did you ever hear who was supposed to get the bucks?" I asked.

"Not officially," Danny said. "But one of the guys involved in the deal told me in the men's room one afternoon that it was supposed to be a lump sum and that the LPGA honcho would parcel it out."

"Who was that?"

"That big broad . . . what's her name? Stilwell. Wynnona Stilwell. She handled all the negotiations. Balls of brass, that one," Danny said, laughing. "I heard she had a list of favored players that she wanted us to present to the network so they could get all the live coverage. Did you ever? Our people took great pleasure in telling her to fuck off, let me tell you."

"Very interesting," I said. "I wonder if other sponsors got the same kind of . . . er . . . opportunity from the LPGA?"

"Oh, hell, I imagine so," Danny said. "Stuff like that's the facts of life, these days," he said. "You wouldn't believe what our football sponsorship program includes. Booze. Bimbos. Skybox seats. Weekends in Vegas. Hell, we probably would've signed on the golf deal, our beloved leader loves the game so."

He was referring to the famous head of his corporation, a man who had turned the company around and made himself famous by starring in most of the company's TV commercials.

"Playing in the pro-am was one of the high points of his life, they tell me," Danny continued. "But he got pissed off that last year when his professional partner wouldn't talk to him during the round. He came back and said he never met such a bitch in his entire life. You know, come to think of it, I think it was that Stilwell woman he played with that year. Huh! Never thought of that before. It fits, though."

"Yeah," I said, "She can be a little tough to get along with."

"I guess so," Danny said. "Tough enough to lose a major tournament sponsor and a corporation with some pretty deep pockets. That's damn tough."

I thanked Danny for the information and rang off. The

shadows of the afternoon had given way to the curtain of dusk. I began to think about dinner: where and with who. As if in answer, there came a knock at my door.

I opened it to find Sybil Montgomery standing there, smiling at me brightly. Her hair was brushed back from her face, which carried the soft sheen of new makeup. She held a magnum of champagne under one arm, and two sparkling crystal glasses.

"I believe the sun has officially descended below the yardarm," she said to me.

"And?" I said, standing in the doorway, keeping her out in the hall.

"And I thought we should get together and celebrate the end of a nice day and having met one another."

"And?"

"And I thought it important to prove to you that not all female professional golfers are . . . er . . . anti-man."

"Well, since this is a scientific inquiry, please come in." I stepped out of the way and bowed her into the room.

Later, after room service had brought dinner, and after we had polished off most of the champagne, and after we had talked and talked and talked, sitting together out on the tiny patio barely big enough to sit on without scraping your knees on the wall . . . after we had watched the twilight deepen from shades of pink and orange into blues and purples and finally into black . . . after we had listened to the city sounds dwindle and fade, to the cicadas begin their nightly chorus of high-pitched vibrations . . . after I had reached out to hold her slender but strong hand in mine in the quiet of the evening, to share the feeling of connection with the cosmos around us . . .

After all of that, we rose as one and went inside. And performed the next part of our scientific experiment. We shed our clothes silently in the cool darkness of the room, leaving the door to the outside open, so that the sounds of the evening world could come inside with us. We were silent as we explored each other's bodies, luminescent in the near darkness, passing hands softly into those fiery secret places, revelling in

115

the tactile sensations that were heightened by the soft caress of the cool evening air flowing gently into the room.

And then we added our own sounds to the dark and quiet world around us as we began our rhythmic pleasures. Slowly, oh, so slowly, then faster, our bodies moved and our breathing quickened. Soft, stolen cries rent the air. Until we both reached the final exhalation, the gentle death, and sank slowly and gratefully back to earth together, warmed and dampened and released and sated.

It was, for me, a necessary thing. A reaffirmation of the good that is in life, and in other creatures. A reminder that all of creation is not bad or evil or wicked. I felt, in those moments before sleep overtook me, reconnected with humanity, with pleasure, with fun. I slept, I am sure, with a smile on my face.

CHAPTER 16

I awoke early, and alone. I sat up and scanned the room, which was empty. I couldn't see any sign of our evening together, save the two empty champagne glasses on the cocktail table. No hurriedly scribbled notes: "Thanks for a good time, ya big lug!" Sighing, I went into the bathroom. No lipstick hearts drawn on the mirror. Empty.

" 'Tis brief, m'lord. As woman's love."

I got on a Shakespeare kick in college, in between golf tournaments, and used to know whole scenes by rote. Don't ask me why . . . It doesn't come in handy much either playing or writing about golf. But I've noticed that bits and pieces come flooding back to me at the oddest times, and one of the oddest is after sex. Like this morning, in the shower, those two lines. *Hamlet* always was a downer.

It was regret, I figured. Not over the act itself, but the briefness of the glow it had produced. There was never enough glow and it never lasted long enough.

I shrugged it off in the steam of the shower, and made ready to face the world anew. It was another golden Florida morning, it was Friday, and the golf tournament, which on the LPGA only runs three days, would begin this morning. Three good reasons for girding one's loins and heading forth.

The telephone interrupted me in mid-gird.

"Hacker?" said a soft voice on the other end. It was Honie Carlton. I slapped my forehead in sudden anguish. My episode with Sybil had pushed all thought of my young friend out of my head. I was immediately, and intensely, guilty.

"Honie," I said. "How are you feeling? Where are you? Are you okay? . . ."

She stopped my rush of words with a tiny laugh.

"Oh, Hacker, shut up and listen," she said. There was a tiny reminder of the pre-attack lilt in her voice. "I'm fine, I'm back at the hotel, my boss came in from Texas and is taking care of me. Now listen. I just heard some news, and you won't believe it. Benton Bergmeister is dead!"

I was, as they say, struck dumb. Bergmeister had faded out of my consciousness that night we had come upon Honie after her attack. In the excitement of getting her to the hospital, and all that followed thereafter, I had forgotten about old Benton. And that he had been about to tell me why he was quitting the LPGA Tour. I guess he really had. Quit, that is.

"Hacker . . . are you there?" Honie demanded petulantly. "Did you hear what I said? Ben—"

"I heard, I heard," I said. "When, where, and how?"

"I don't know. I just overheard Karla—she's my boss who just flew in—talking to someone. She just ran out of here all afluster, so I figure they must have just found out."

"Thanks, kid," I said. "I'm on the case. Anything you need?"

"Naw," she said. "Go get 'em."

I got. In the lobby, there was no outward manifestation of anything abnormal going on. People were coming out of elevators, heading for the restaurant, sitting in chairs reading newspapers, booking tours with the concierge. Normal American life, resort-hotel style.

Behind the desk, the hotel staffers were also going about their business. Except for one young girl, with pretty blond hair, who was standing over to one side, almost out of sight. Her face had gone pure white, and she held a hand over her mouth in the traditional pose of shock. I watched as an older man in a gray suit wandered past her, stopping to whisper something urgently in her ear. She immediately shook her head and jumped back to work, picking up a stack of papers and heading for the nearest computer terminal.

But that told me that something unusual was afoot.

I headed immediately to the security trailer. When I walked in, Don Collier was speaking frantically on the telephone. He hung up as soon as he saw me walk in.

"Hey, Don," I said as pleasantly as possible. "Where's the stiff?"

He stared at me. "Where? . . . Who? . . . How?" he started three different questions, almost together.

I laughed. "Word travels fast," I said, "Especially amongst us newshounds. So what's the scoop?"

He sighed, deeply. One of the telephones on his desk began an insistent chirping. He flipped it a bird and jumped up out of his chair.

"Fuck it," he growled. "I'm tired of talking with these PR types. C'mon. You might as well come with me. You seem to know it all anyway."

He led me back into the hotel, to the north wing, to the third floor. Benton Bergmeister had been assigned an "inside room," which was a euphemistic way of saying he had been given a parking-lot view. Oh, the view featured nice landscaping, and away in the distance was the Olympic-size swimming pool surrounded by lush flowering beds, but it still overlooked a parking lot. Big Wyn had the palatial suite, and the poor commish, who had the misfortune of possessing a dick, got the parking-lot room.

Benton's room was occupied by about a half-dozen plain-clothes cops, all of whom seemed to be doing officious things. All of whom totally ignored the body of Benton Bergmeister lying on his bed, naked and sagging, on his back, one arm by his side, the other flung casually across his pale and flaccid belly. He looked, as do most dead naked people, smaller,

119

somewhat shrunken. His eyes were closed, his mouth slightly ajar, as if he had been caught in midsnore. In fact, he looked asleep. In a nap that would apparently last forever.

The room was neat and clean. Bergmeister's briefcase lay on the desk, open, with papers spilling out. Next to the briefcase was a bottle of Scotch, empty save for about two inches in the bottom. There were no clothes scattered about the room, I noticed, which struck me as odd considering the fact that Benton's body was nude. I guess he was a neat stiff.

One of the cops saw us and walked over.

"Hey, Don," he said, "we're about done here. Who's this?"

"Hacker," Collier answered. The cop looked at me with flat, penetrating, clear gray eyes. "He's a golf writer doing a story on the ladies' Tour."

"Well, I guess he's got himself something to write about," the cop said. He motioned toward the body of Benton Bergmeister on the bed, silent in its eternity.

"What happened?" I asked.

"Guy died," the cop said and walked away.

"Friendly people here in Miami," I said loudly to Collier. "I thought all the assholes in the world lived in Boston."

The smart-ass cop turned around sharply at that, and Collier hustled me out of the bedroom into the hall.

"Cause of death?" I asked.

"They're not sure," Collier said, and sighed. "Hopefully it's a heart attack, or stroke, or something natural."

"Yeah, that'd get the monkey off the hotel's back," I said.

"Cynical, yeah, but true," Collier agreed. "It might also be suicide. In addition to the bottle of booze, there were a whole lot of prescription bottles in the guy's bathroom kit, and a lot of them were empty or nearly gone. One of the dicks said that mixing some of those pills with all the booze woulda been a no-no—a quiet but effective way to go."

"Inconvenient," I said. "But again, the hotel's off the hot seat. But maybe someone offed old Benton."

"Shit, Hacker," Collier said. "Don't even think that! You saw that room. There wasn't the first hint of foul play in there.

120

Guy took off his clothes, hung them up, laid down on the bed, and expired. One way or another."

The smart-ass cop came out into the hallway and lit a cigarette. He blew out the smoke silently while he affixed those gray eyes on Collier and I.

"M.E. on the way?" Collier asked. The cop nodded. His eyes never moved. "Well, let me know what he says. I got an entire front office ready to shit themselves. Not good on the publicity front."

The cop shrugged. I could tell that he wasn't going to stay up nights worrying about what problems the executives of the Doral Hotel and Country Club might have on the publicity front.

"Listen," I said to the cop. "I don't know if it means anything or not, but a couple of nights ago, Bergmeister told me he was getting ready to quit his job."

The cop looked at me with a hint of interest this time. "That right?" he asked, letting more smoke waft out of his nostrils.

"Yeah," I said. "And my impression was that he was damn glad to be getting out of here. I think he was tired of working for a bunch of women."

"I can understand that," the cop said as he turned to go back into the bedroom. "Working for fuckin' women'll kill ya."

CHAPTER 17

Don Collier promised to let me know later what the medical examiner had to say about the cause of Benton Bergmeister's death. I headed for the tournament pressroom, where about ten fellow members of the Fourth Estate had gathered to report on the tournament's first round, which was just getting underway.

I could see where Honie had her work cut out for her. On a typical first-round day at the typical PGA Tour event, there would be at least thirty reporters, writers, and photographers hanging around. By the weekend, that number would, at a minimum, double, depending on the size of the city in which the tournament was played. Now, Miami is a pretty big media market, but only ten sportswriters had stirred themselves to attend the big doings at the women's golf tournament. Actually, only eight. The two I knew who were national reporters were Barley Raney from the Associated Press and Penny Schoenfeld, a stringer for *Golf World*.

Barley is an old but happy drunk. Short and heavy-set, his face is a riot of capillary explosions, like someone had taken his face and shoved it against a plate glass window a hundred times. His heyday in the golf-writing business had been the sixties: the Ascension of "King Jack" and the Fall of the House of Palmer. Now, though probably well over retirement age, Barley Raney was hanging on, stringing his way around the country for the AP, pounding out his thirty graphs week after week after week. He simply didn't know what else to do with his life.

Penny covered maybe a dozen women's events for the weekly golf magazine. I think she married somebody rich, and really didn't work for money, just for a chance to get out of the house. Her means of escape was covering golf, which she usually did in the comfort of the air-conditioned clubhouse. I saw her try to play golf one year down in Myrtle Beach, and I don't want to see that again . . . ever.

The rest of the "crowd" were local reporters—some TV, mostly print. They sat around as if waiting for something to happen. Out on the course, the early tee times featured the Tour's younger and not-yet-famous players. The LPGA always heavily weights the later tee times with the better players, since fans usually come out around midday.

At the front of the room, a telephone glued to her ear, sat an attractive woman in her midforties. She wore a nice blue dress with a fashionable scarf affixed jauntily to one shoulder. A string of pearls and some dangly earrings completed the picture. This must be the Karla person that Honie had mentioned to me. Her boss, fresh in from Texas.

"Say," I yelled loudly toward the front of the room. "Are you gonna have a press conference or just release a statement about Benton Bergmeister?"

The lady in the blue dress looked up in some surprise, murmured something into her telephone, and hung up.

One of the TV guys—he had a very nice tan—looked over at me.

"Who's this Bergmisher?"

"Bergmeister," I said, still speaking loud enough for everyone to hear. "He's the commissioner of the LPGA. Or, was, anyway. He just croaked. The police are crawling around his stiff right now."

"No shit?" the TV guy yelled. He jumped to a telephone and began to frantically dial. The other reporters all came to attention. Several turned to the blue dress at the front of the room and began to shout questions at her.

I just smiled. Hacker kicks over the beehive again. A role I am most justly famous for, if I do say so myself.

"Now, hold on, hold on," the lady was saying, holding her hands out. "I'm not hiding anything. I was about to make an announcement, but I wanted to hear the latest facts from the police before I said anything."

"Bullshit, lady," yelled Barley Raney. "You was holdin' out on us. C'mon, give."

The lady sighed. "All we know is that Benton Bergmeister was found dead in his room this morning. The police are investigating, and will be releasing information later concerning the cause of death."

"Karla . . . was there foul play involved?" asked Penny Schoenfeld.

"We have no indication of any foul play at this time," said Karla.

"Do you think the fact that Benton Bergmeister was about to resign as commissioner of the LPGA had any bearing on his death?" I asked. Innocently and sweetly, I gave the hive another swift kick.

Karla was nonplussed for a minute, but, being the true PR type that she was, she quickly recovered.

"I don't know where you got that information," she said, "but I suggest you double-check it to make sure it's not pure rumor and innuendo."

Slick, I thought. She dodged the question without answering it straight out. Old Edward L. Bernays, the Father of American Public Relations, would be proud of this one. Trouble was, Barley Raney, besotted or not, had been around PR types for decades, and he, too, noticed the slightly askew answer.

"C'mon lady, it's getting hip-deep in here," he growled.

124

"Was 'Bergy' in or out? Guy was always fun to drink with."

Karla the PR lady paused to frame her answer.

"Benton Bergmeister was scheduled to retire in two years," she said carefully, "when he reached the mandatory retirement age. There had been some discussions between Benton and the Tour about an early retirement, but as far as I know, no final decisions had been reached."

Barley looked over at me and winked. "He was out," he said, and reached for his telephone.

"Now, hold on," said Karla, a worried look on her face. "I insist that you act responsibly in this matter, and not resort to printing half-truths and rumor without verification. I would hope that as professional journalists, you would await the facts in this matter and not—"

"Professional journalists, my ass," boomed a voice from the back of the room. "They ain't nothing but a bunch of rewrite men."

We all turned to see Big Wyn Stilwell making her way up to the interview stage at the front of the room. She was dressed for golf, in a loud pink checked outfit.

"Hey, Wyn," said Barley Raney, "You gotta comment on Bergmeister?"

"Well, yes, Barley, as a matter of fact, I do," Wyn said, and she perched on the edge of the table. Karla the PR lady, her face showing immense relief at having a greater authority taking command of the situation, shrank into the background like good PR people do.

"I have had the pleasure of knowing and working with Benton Bergmeister for the last five years," Wyn said. Her face was earnest and serious in mien. "I was shocked to hear of his death this morning, and I know all the players share my dismay and sense of loss. Benton Bergmeister did great work for the Ladies' Professional Golf Tour, and his time and talents will be sorely missed."

It was a perfect speech. Hit just the right notes. A performance of bravura and bullshit. All the press lemmings were writing down every word she said. Time for another kick to the beehive.

125

"Is it true that Bergmeister had discussed his resignation with you two days ago?" I asked.

Big Wyn smiled evilly in my direction.

"Absolutely not," she said grimly.

"Was he depressed about the management of the Tour, especially the level of control exercised over the day-to-day affairs of the tour by the players' committee?" I asked sweetly. Out of the corner of my eye I could see Barley Raney snap to attention. I'm sure he had never heard a question like that addressed to Big Wyn Stilwell.

A couple of dangerous-looking red spots appeared high on Big Wyn's cheekbones. But, give her credit, she kept her anger bottled inside.

"Benton Bergmeister never said anything of that kind directly to me," she said slowly. "I guess you'll have to ask the other members of the committee if he said anything to them."

"So to your knowledge, Bergmeister was not depressed about his job and ready to quit?" I concluded.

"No," Big Wyn said, and I saw her eyes narrow as she suddenly understood what I was doing.

I knew before I asked my questions what her answers would be. But in asking those kinds of questions, I had put a bug in the ears of my fellow reporters. All of them were suddenly turning the import of my line of questioning over in their minds. Benton Bergmeister may have been depressed, or angry, or upset with the leadership of the LPGA. His death may have been the result of those feelings. Suddenly, Benton Bergmeister's death was not just an unfortunate occurrence, but could have been linked to conditions of his job, conditions that could still exist. That was interesting and might be worth pursuing.

Big Wyn understood all of this, and knew she had to do some damage control, and quick.

"Benton's health had not been the best in the last few months," she said, looking at me coldly. "He and I had talked some time ago about the possibility of his retiring early for that reason. I told Benton that we needed his services, but that of course his first responsibility was to himself, his family, and

126

his health and that we would understand if he felt he was jeopardizing his health in any way. He had been feeling better of late, and so the subject had not come up, but—"

Big Wyn broke off and cast her eyes downward. It was a bravura performance, if it was a performance, and all of us in the room felt the emotion.

"Did he have a family?" I asked after a minute.

Big Wyn's head came up, and she looked at me again. This time, I saw, for a fleeting instant, a predator's glint in her eyes. The glint of victory that's there when the kill has been completed, and the prey lies in the grass, bleeding from wounds of throat and viscera, eyes open but unseeing, waiting to be devoured. It was the briefest of flashes, that glint I saw in her eyes. But in those nanoseconds, I heard the plaintive howling across the snowy plains, the primitive breast-beating, the thump of the victory drums through the darkest of the jungle nights.

"He was married once," was all she said. "But he was divorced some years ago. I believe he had a daughter."

That's all she said. But the remembrance of that look sent chills racing up and down my spine.

CHAPTER 18

About an hour later, we had a mimeographed obituary of Benton Bergmeister in hand, courtesy of the LPGA. It didn't mention his heavy drinking, nor his stated intention to resign from his post. We had all been busy filing stories on Bergmeister's demise and what it would mean to the Tour. I was probably the only one who questioned, in my story, the appropriateness of the ladies' Tour continuing to stage its tournament, but I knew my editor would take it out. He understands that a simple death will never get in the way of American commerce. If the NFL could play games two days after JFK's assassination, the LPGA could certainly shoulder on.

Before breaking for lunch, I decided to head out to the practice range and get some reaction quotes from some of the players. My route took me through the main lobby of the hotel. I ran into Honie Carlton, wearing a turban-style bandage, who was talking with an elderly lady who was improbably wearing a light cardigan draped over her shoulders. It was probably ninety-two degrees outside in the bright sunshine.

"Hacker!" Honie cried when she saw me. I trudged over slowly. "Hacker, this is Ethel Burbank," she said. "She is . . . er was, Benton's secretary back at headquarters."

I looked at the woman. She was in her late fifties, it appeared, with silvery, wispy hair pushed back from her face. Horn-rimmed spectacles hung on a string from her neck, where they banged against her formidable bosom when she moved. She was obviously distraught: She clutched a damp tissue in one hand, and dark red splotches danced across her face.

"How do you do," I said politely. "I'm sorry about your boss."

"Yes, yes, oh, yes, terrible," she exclaimed rapidly, waving her hand about in the air distractedly. "I heard about it just as I was finishing my breakfast! What a tragedy! Such a dear, dear man!"

"Ethel has worked with Benton for more than ten years," Honie explained to me. "They were a real team."

"Oh, that poor, dear man," Ethel began to sob, dabbing at her eyes with her tissue. Honie wrapped her arms around the woman and hugged her. She looked at me over the woman's head and rolled her eyes.

"Miss Burbank," I said gently. The woman looked up at me with teary eyes. "When did you last speak to Benton?"

"Well now, let me see," she said, mostly to herself. But I noted a sharpness and a focus return to her eyes. Ethel Burbank was nobody's fool.

"Why, I spoke to him several times yesterday," she answered. "We always conversed first thing in the morning, taking care of the usual daily detail work. But he called me back later in the morning and asked me to fly right down to Miami. He said he needed my help in preparing something."

"Do you often come out on tour?" I asked.

"Very rarely, dear," she said, nodding at me. "I really have enough to do back at headquarters. But Benton said it was important, that he . . . he needed me."

She began to weep again.

I waited until she composed herself again.

"Do you remember what it was he needed?" I asked.

"He didn't really tell me, dearie," she said apologetically, laying a withered hand on my arm. "I think . . . yes, I remember. He said he had to prepare some things to present to the players' committee. He didn't give me any more details. Frankly, I thought he was just making something up to give me an excuse to fly down here. Benton knew how much I love going to the racetrack."

As that thought came to her, she broke down anew in a fresh bout of tears. Honie, bless her nurturing heart, put her arms around the woman and cried with her.

I stood there thinking while they wept, smiling inanely at the curious stares of the tourists traversing the lobby. In a minute or two they were done.

"Miss Burbank, may I ask just one more question?" I began. Wiping her eyes with her drenched hanky, she nodded.

"Did anyone else here in Miami know you were coming?" I asked. "I mean, anyone from the LPGA."

She fixed me with a level gaze, her eyes liquid but sharp.

"Why, no, dearie," she said, "I don't believe so. Except for Miss Casey, of course. I called her to book me a flight and arrange a room. She's our travel expert, don'cha know?"

Honie and I looked at each other for a moment. Then Honie bundled the woman off somewhere. I stood and watched them go, thinking.

Casey Carlyle, the Delicious One, Big Wyn's eyes and ears, had known that Benton Bergmeister had called for his secretary. I had no doubt that she had asked why Ethel was coming to Miami, and I had no doubt that the garrulous Ethel had told her what she told me. That Benton needed some help in preparing something to present to the players' committee. So, Big Wyn must have known that something was up.

Had she confronted Bergmeister and scared him to death? It would not be a wild assumption, after everything I had learned about the woman during the past few days. Or had Benton's body conveniently given out at just the right time? Or was there some kind of foul play involved?

130

I quickly shook my head. Jumping to farfetched conclusions there, I told myself.

Out on the practice range, a dozen players were striking balls preparing for the day's first round. Already, I knew, some twenty threesomes had teed off, both from the first and tenth holes; this process would continue until midafternoon.

Down at the far corner of the range, I spied Mary Beth Burke talking beside the water cooler with Sybil Montgomery. I made a beeline.

"Hullo, ladies," I said as I walked up. "I need some suitably morose quotes about Benton Bergmeister for tomorrow's paper."

"Quit, Hacker," Burkey chastised me. "I thought he was a nice old guy. It's real sad."

"Right," I echoed. "Nice guy. Real sad. Sybil? Got anything to add to that?"

She stared back at me seriously, not playing my game. "How did it happen, Hacker?" she asked. "What killed the man?"

"Don't know," I told them. "There'll be an autopsy, but for now the police are assuming the guy just croaked."

I saw Mary Beth and Sybil exchange a glance.

"Frankly," I continued, "it sounds just a hair too neat and clean for me. I mean, Benton told me two days ago he was about to quit, then he called his secretary to come to Miami and help prepare some kind of papers for the players' committee . . . and then he dies. That's pretty damn convenient of him, at least as far as Big Wyn is concerned. From what I gathered, Benton was feeling like singing about something Big Wyn did to him."

The two women exchanged that look again.

"So I'm thinking there's got to be something below the surface going on," I continued, in a breezy, conversational tone. "And from what I've learned about this operation in the last few days, it doesn't surprise me in the least that that something might be subterranean and nasty. And watching

131

you two guys give each other the secret high sign, I figure you might know what it is."

They looked at each other a third time, then turned back to me blank-faced.

"I don't know what you're talking about," Burkey said calmly.

"Bullshit," I exploded. "We all know how Big Wyn works, and we all know that she had some kind of hold on Bergmeister from which he somehow got the balls to break loose. I don't know what that hold was, and you do. So give."

They looked at each other one more time. Sybil gave Burkey the slightest nod of approval.

"Well, Hacker, we don't know exactly what she had on the guy either," Burkey told me. "All we know is the rumor that's been around as long as Benton was commish. It could be true, or it could be rumor. That's up to you to decide."

"Okay," I said. "That's fair. What was it?"

Mary Beth sighed. "Well, the word was that Benton got caught in some kind of sexual fling with one of the rookies in his first year on the job. She was a real young rookie, too, they said, which got him in extra-hot water. The word is that Big Wyn buried the whole escapade and put Benton's balls in her pocketbook."

"Do you know who this young player was?" I asked. "Is she still playing today? Where does she live?"

I could smell the story now, and like a hunting dog after the coon, I was suddenly whipped into a high fever of excitement. There were no fences too high, no thickets too thick to prevent me from sniffing my way to the lair and howling to the sky the secret of my discovery.

Burkey shook her head. "Nope," she said. "Neither of us ever heard a name to go with the story. Could be there isn't one. Could be the story was made up in the first place."

"Well, I'll just have to do some digging," I said, mostly to myself. "Somebody's got to know something."

"Hold on, Hacker," Sybil said. "You're leaping the hedgerow without your mount. I shouldn't think you'll have much luck running amok around here trying to dig up some ancient

132

dirt. We tend to band together in the face of such. I think you'd best let Mary Beth and I muck about quietly and see if we can uncover the name of the unlucky lass in this alleged episode. Don't you agree, Mary Beth?" she asked.

"That's A-one right," Burkey agreed. "If anybody does know anything, they're more likely to confide some gossip to Sybil here or me than to some wise-ass male reporter who's a goddamn Yankee to boot."

"Here, here," Sybil echoed. They stared at me mockingly, faint smiles playing at the corners of both their mouths.

"Damn, it's hard being a man," I said.

Their peals of laughter rang out over the peaceful green fairways.

CHAPTER 19

I noticed a good-size gallery gathering around the first tee and strolled over to see who was about to begin her round. There was a young tournament volunteer holding a sign on a pole that had the names of the three players in the group about to tee off. Rosie Jones, a perennially tough competitor on the LPGA Tour, was one of the names on the board, along with Ellen Russon, a young player I knew absolutely nothing about. The third name was Wynnona Stilwell.

I elbowed my way through the crowd to stand at the ropes next to the tee box. Rosie was standing there, staring off down the fairway in rapt concentration. The young Miss Russon, a pretty girl with golden brown hair, stood nervously by her caddy, swishing a club back and forth and glancing occasionally at her watch.

The tournament starter was also getting nervous. He wore a broad-brimmed Panama hat against the Florida sun and a short-sleeved white shirt. He studied his clipboard, glanced at his watch, and kept scanning the crowd for Big Wyn, who was nowhere to be found.

"Big Wyn's not here," I heard someone in the crowd murmur. "She's supposed to be in the one thirty-two group. Where is she?"

"Could be a scratch," another fan answered. "If she doesn't show up before the group tees off, she's disqualified."

The rumor of Big Wyn's possible disqualification rushed through the crowd around the tee like wildfire. Rosie Jones ignored the hubbub, as she continued to stand, arms akimbo, looking off in rapt concentration down the first fairway. The other young golfer whispered to her caddy, grinned, and shrugged her shoulders. She apparently didn't mind not playing against a living legend.

The tournament starter looked at his watch one more time, shook his head sadly, and picked up an electronic megaphone to announce the players in the group.

It was just at that moment that the crowd of fans parted as if on cue, and a determined-looking Wynnona Stilwell marched out onto the tee, followed by her caddy. The crowd burst into loud applause and seemed to heave a common sigh of relief.

I realized, suddenly, that the timing of her appearance had been contrived. It was a small psych game, her waiting until near-disqualification to appear. It let her opponents know that Big Wyn was the star—one who could, and would, push the rules to the outer limit and get away with it.

Big Wyn strode around the tee, shaking hands with the officials and at least one of her opponents. Ellen Russon had visibly blanched when she saw Big Wyn stride onto the tee, going white, then red in the face. She bravely shook Big Wyn's proffered hand, but it was apparent that the episode had somewhat unnerved the girl. Rosie Jones, on the other hand, never blinked, or moved, or even acknowledged that Big Wyn had arrived. She maintained her steely visage and her pose of staring down the fairway until the introductions began.

"Ladies and gentlemen," the starter pronounced, his voice a tinny echo through his megaphone, "The one thirty-two group. From Bolton, Vermont, in her second year on tour, Ellen Russon." The crowd gave the girl a polite hand, which she acknowledged with a friendly wave. "From San Diego, California, in her twelfth year on Tour, seven-time winner, Rosie Jones!" The applause was much louder. Rosie had her own fan club in attendance. She was busy storing something in a pocket of her golf bag, but finally held up a hand to acknowledge the applause.

"And finally, a golfer who needs no introduction. A resident of Phoenix, Arizona, thirty-two tournament victories, former U.S. Women's Open and U.S. Amateur champion, and truly one of golf's legendary figures, Big Wyn Stilwell!"

The burst of noise split through the humid air. It was a solid wall of sound, accentuated with whistles and cheers, and it lasted at least three minutes. Big Wyn reveled in it. She removed her visor and waved it high above her head, and when the sound and cheering continued, she threw back her head and laughed aloud. Big Wyn Stilwell was in her element, at the top of her world, basking in adulation.

It was right about then that she caught sight of me, standing against the ropes. I was not clapping, or cheering, or whistling. I had my arms crossed, and I was staring at her. I'm sure she read on my face what I was thinking, because I saw her eyes narrow and her face darken. We locked eyes, and in that moment, we were gladiators facing off in the Coliseum; knights about to begin a joust; linemen on opposite sides of the line of scrimmage at the Super Bowl. There were hatred and a duel to the death contained in our look.

The rest of the crowd must have noticed the change in Big Wyn and assumed she was beginning her concentration on the task at hand, for they fell slowly silent. Ellen Russon had the honor, and she prepared to tee off.

"Go on, honey," Big Wyn said in a rather too loud voice. "Show us what you got."

Ellen shot Big Wyn an angry glance. She did not appreciate the condescending tone, nor the rather bald attempt at further psychological warfare. Some in the crowd chuckled.

Her drive was a fine one, but it drifted a bit right and finished well down the fairway in the first cut of rough. She was rewarded with a loud round of applause, and I could see her shoulders heave with relief. The first one is always the toughest.

Rosie Jones, who had still not spoken or looked at her opponents, was next. Big Wyn knew better than to try a blatant psych job on her. Mechanically, Jones teed her ball, stood behind it while she envisioned the shot, then stepped up to the ball and launched a beautiful drive that split the fairway. She, too, was rewarded by the fans with loud applause.

As Big Wyn prepared to hit her drive, the fans could not contain themselves. "C'mon, Wyn!" yelled one. "Do it, Momma!" cried another.

Stilwell teed her ball, then strode over to her caddy, selected her driver, and took a couple of practice swings. She was frozen in address, preparing to launch into her swing, when someone right behind me took her picture. The distinctive, high-pitched whine of a camera's motorized advance drive filled the deadly silence.

Big Wyn stepped back from her ball and glared in my direction. I smiled at her.

"Goddamn it," she snarled at the tournament official standing nearby. "That son of a bitch did that on purpose. I want his press credentials confiscated and his sorry butt thrown out of here!"

Her outburst stunned the crowd. The tournament official turned white and strode over to the ropes where I stood. I continued smiling as I held my hands up. Empty.

" 'Tweren't me, Wyn," I said gaily. "Nice try, though."

Behind me, I heard a quavering voice. "I-I-I'm sorry. I didn't realize . . ." We all turned around and saw a red-faced older man, clutching his camera to his chest.

"There are no cameras allowed on the course during the tournament," the official told the man sternly. He turned to Big Wyn, who was still glaring at me, shrugged at her, then held up his hand. "Quiet, please," he called.

Big Wyn slammed her driver head on the turf in frustration. She threw one last vituperative look my way before turning again to the task at hand. But I could tell her concentration wasn't focused on golf: It still lingered on the incident of the

137

camera. And her shot reflected it: It hooked badly down the left side and caught a fairway bunker tucked behind some palms. A bad start.

The crowd murmured in sympathy. "That's okay, Wyn," yelled her loudest fan. "You can do it."

She looked at me again before she headed off down the fairway. I was still grinning. I hoped I looked like Banquo's ghost. I hoped that every time she prepared to swing, she would see my grinning face in her mind's eye.

Big Wyn spat, very unladylike, in my direction, turned, and stalked away.

CHAPTER 20

Most of the fans that had crowded around the first tee followed Big Wyn and the other golfers down the first fairway. I fielded a few dirty looks from some of Wyn's staunchest followers. Obviously, any enemy of Wyn's was an enemy of theirs. I smiled back at them.

Once the crowd had gone, there were only about a dozen people left. Looking across the tee, I saw Harold Stilwell standing in the meager shade of a palm tree, wiping his brow with a handkerchief. He was dressed in his denim coveralls and a white T-shirt, looking every inch the country mechanic he had once been, and he was staring thoughtfully down the fairway at the crowd that was chasing after the fast-striding form of his wife.

I sauntered over to his tree, and when he felt me standing next to him, he looked up at me.

"Buy you a beer?" I asked.

"You do, and I'll be your friend for life," was his reply, and we headed for the nearest concession stand.

I glanced at the main scoreboard as we skirted the eigh-

139

teenth green. Patty Sheehan and Beth Daniel were tied for the lead at four under, and both were still on the back nine somewhere. Betsy King wasn't far behind, and Maggie Wills, a coltish young blonde from Florida, was also hanging around the lead.

I paid five dollars for two luke-cold plastic cups of beer, and we found a table with an umbrella that afforded a little bit of shade, but not much relief from the hot midafternoon sun.

We sipped our beers in silence for a while, watching the other people doing the same. Echoes of cheers and applause drifted over us from faraway holes out on the golf course. I felt that peculiar charged atmosphere that accompanies a professional golf tournament. It's created, I believe, by the unnatural stillness and silences that the fans adopt before a player makes a shot. There's something about that collective holding of breath that makes the air crystalline and brilliant, and the subsequent bursts of cheers and applause sound so loud and ringing. It is an atmospheric condition I have felt at no other sporting event.

I looked over at Stilwell.

"You follow Big Wyn on the course a lot?" I asked.

He started, sitting a bit more upright, as if my words had startled him out of some kind of reverie.

"Wha—? Oh, well, sometimes yes, sometimes, no," he said. "I usually don't bother going out to watch her first round any more. If she's in the thing on Sunday, I like to be there."

"Does she know you're there?"

He grunted, once.

"Wynnona Stilwell knows everything about everything that's going on around her," he said with a small, sad smile. "She's concentrating on her golf for sure, but she can come off the course and tell people to go fix the broken gallery ropes on fifteen, and move the johnnies on seven back a bit, and there's a wet spot on twelve that should be marked 'ground under repair.'" He took a long sip of his beer, leaving a foamy mustache on his upper lip. "I don't know how she does it, but she does. So to answer your question, yes, she knows when I'm there."

He looked out at the passing crowd again.

"She seemed to be in a peculiar kind of mood today," he said musingly. "I dunno, kind of preoccupied. I don't expect she'll play very well. I've seen her like this before."

"Maybe it's Benton's death that's got her down," I suggested.

"Could be, could be," Harold nodded. "Too bad 'bout ole Bergy. Kind of a dandy, and he drank too damn much, but I liked the man. Too bad."

"Did you know him very well?" I asked.

"Nah, not really," he said. "Bergy really didn't come to a whole lot of tournaments. And when he did, he mostly kept to himself. Especially after—"

Stilwell stopped abrupted, catching himself.

"After what?" I asked. "What happened to him?"

Harold Stilwell took another long swallow of beer. He put his cup back on the table, slowly, then turned and looked at me. He shook his head, back and forth. I got the message. He wasn't going to tell me.

"Did he ever say anything to you about resigning? About being upset with . . . the way things were being run?" I knew better than to personalize the question. Harold Stilwell was a loyal husband, and wouldn't take kindly to accusations, even second-hand ones, about his wife.

"Nah," Stilwell shook his head. "Like I said, he didn't talk to me much over the years. Well, once, it's been quite a few years ago, he came to me and started to complain about something Wynnona had decided. I sat that boy down and told him I was a retired man, and did not work for the LPGA in any capacity whatsoever, and that if he had a problem with the LPGA, he should bring it up with someone who worked there." Stilwell smiled. "He got the message, I guess, because he never troubled me with anything but small talk again."

It was my turn to drink some beer. I kept running into these steel doors slamming shut. Stilwell knew what hold Big Wyn had had on Benton Bergmeister, but wasn't telling.

Stilwell interrupted my reverie.

"Tell me, Hacker, you ever wished you could be somebody

141

else?" he asked me suddenly, leaning over the table. "You know, just kinda melt into the crowd, disappear, and come out as somebody new? Start over . . . new life . . . doin' something else? You ever feel that way?"

"Well—" I started.

" 'Cause I sure do, sometimes," he finished.

I thought carefully. This was new ground, and I wanted to step carefully. There might be buried mines here, or buried treasure.

"I suppose," I said, "if I was living a life that was pretty strictly run by somebody else, I might feel like running away sometimes."

"Damn right," Stilwell nodded.

"But I've always tried to make sure nobody else was pulling on my strings," I said. "I like to handle that part myself."

Stilwell was silent, staring out at the people.

"I would think," I continued, "that if I was in a situation where someone else was in control, and I didn't like it, I would be able to do something about it, short of running away. There are lots of ways to skin a cat, as they say."

Harold Stilwell mumbled something.

"What?"

"Mumbo jumbo," he said. "Bunch a damn mumbo jumbo."

We lapsed again into silence as I turned things over in my mind. We were sitting in an area between the eighteenth green and the clubhouse behind us. Suddenly, out of the milling crowd, Julie Warren appeared. Visibly sweaty and trailed by her caddy, she had obviously just finished her round and was heading for the clubhouse. Almost at the same moment, she caught sight of Harold and I sitting there together, and I could see her eyes narrow.

She whirled and headed straight for us. A little girl clutching a white sun visor and a ballpoint pen crossed her path and held the items up, asking for an autograph. Julie Warren growled something at the girl and shook her head sternly. The little girl turned away with a look of shock and surprise on her face.

Julie Warren strode directly up to our table.

"Hal, I don't think you should be talking with this guy," she said to Stilwell, making a rude thumb gesture at me. "I don't think Big Wyn would like it."

Stilwell leaned back in his chair, hooked his thumbs in his coveralls, and cocked his head back to look at her.

"I happen to be enjoyin' a cold brew with my friend here," he said in an exaggerated drawl, nodding briefly in my direction. "If it's any business of yours, which it ain't."

"He's out to get us, you old fart," she cried. "I'm telling you, don't talk to him!"

Harold Stilwell leaped to his feet and put his suddenly red and angry face right next to hers.

"And I'm tellin' you to mind your own goddamn business," he growled, his voice low and dangerous.

They stayed in the position, eyes locked, for several long seconds.

"I'm telling Big Wyn," she said.

"I'm supposed to pee my pants?" he inquired. "Go on, get oughta here."

Julie Warren turned on her heel and stomped away. She didn't look at me, which is too bad, because I had on my best innocent angel face.

"Lovely woman," I said as she left.

"Class A bitch," Harold muttered.

I couldn't disagree, so I bought him another beer.

Thirty minutes later, I was heading for the pressroom to see if Sheehan or Daniels had been caught by anybody.

Sybil Montgomery intercepted me. She was heading for the first tee, her caddy in tow, ready to begin her first round. She slowed when she saw me and allowed the caddy to walk on by. With one hand aloft, she waved me over. I went.

She rested her hand lightly on my shoulder, and her eyes fastened on mine. Quietly, with a pleasant smile playing faintly about her lips, she whispered a name to me.

"Cindy D'Angelo," she said, and winked.

"Dinner tonight?" I answered. She laughed, her eyes dancing.

"Sounds perfectly lovely," she answered. "I'll have to let you know. Tah-tah, dahling."

With a final wave, she strode off toward the first tee, her office, with her afternoon's work ahead. I watched her go, and felt the place where her hand had rested on my shoulder tingle. It was a nice feeling, that tingle. I wanted more of it.

Sighing, I headed on to the blessed relief of the pressroom, grabbed a beer out of the cooler, and plopped down in an empty chair. I took my time drinking while I studied early results being posted on the scoreboard. Daniel was one ahead of Sheehan, with a half-dozen others within four shots. Big Wyn had just bogeyed the eighth, I saw, and was now three over for the day. I smiled happily.

When Honie Carlton walked into the room, I motioned her over, then got up and led her to a quiet, out-of-the-way corner of the big room. I didn't want to be overheard.

"Need some research, kid," I said to her. "Former player named Cindy D'Angelo. Rookie about ten years ago, probably very young, as in teens. I'd like to know about her and where she is today, if possible."

"Okay," Honie said.

"And, Honie, keep this very, very quiet," I said seriously. "I mean top secret. It could be dangerous if certain people find out what I'm doing."

She fingered the bandage wrapped around her head.

"You got it," she said, turned on her heel, and left.

God, I love to delegate. Especially when they obey your commands. I felt good enough, having set some wheels in motion, to get another beer from the cooler and make it last at least five minutes. Like the others I had already consumed, it went down exceedingly smoothly.

I placed a call to Don Collier, who told me that Bergmeister's autopsy was scheduled for sometime that afternoon. But, he said, the police had put Bergmeister's death down to natural and as-yet-unknown causes and closed the file.

"Guy got any family?" I asked.

"One daughter is all," Collier said. "She asked to have his effects packed up and sent out to her in California. Someone

144

from the tour did all that this morning. I'm still trying to recover from the experience."

"How's that?"

"Let me put it this way," Collier said, chuckling. "Hubba-hubba to the nth degree."

"Oh, that must have been Casey," I said. "Did she bat her long eyelashes at you?"

"No, dammit," Collier growled. "I had to make an inventory list of all Bergmeister's belongings as she packed them up, but she was as cold and efficient as a stiletto."

"Yeah, I've, ah, heard she can be tough to crack," I said, trying not to laugh.

"But I can see where some might want to give their all in the attempt, though," Collier said, and rang off.

Barley Raney strolled over and perched his hip on the side of my desk.

"So, Hacker," he boomed at me. "How do you like covering the ladies? You gonna defect and make this a full-time gig?"

I laughed.

"Hell, Barley," I said. "Way too much politics and back-stabbing going on for my tastes. In the men's game, all they do is play golf."

Barley nodded sadly.

"Yeah, I know what you mean," he said. "Get on the wrong side of somebody here, you get awful tee times, guaranteed spike-marked greens, or early morning times with lots of dew still on the grass. But you know what I hate the most?"

He screwed up his face in a look of intense disgust.

I waited.

"They're all so goddamn nice to each other in public," he told me. " 'Oh, little Suzy just played so great today . . . I'm so happy for her,' they'll say, when you know they want to take a three-iron and wrap it completely around little Suzy's freakin' head."

Barley sighed.

"I wish just once one of 'em would say something like, 'I goddamn choked my guts out there and I'm so goddamn mad

145

at lil Suzy over there that I'd like to take this putter and cram it up—"

I interrupted Barley's fantasy with my laughter.

Honie Carlton strode back into the pressroom, a big grin creasing her face. We went back into the somewhat quiet corner.

"Computers are wonderful things," she told me. "They know everything."

"Give."

"She played on tour for just three years," Honie told me. "Quit about six years ago. Never won much money. Was, like you suggested, very young, only eighteen when she turned pro. Probably burned out fast."

"Yeah, that fits," I said. "Where was she from?"

"Florida." Honie smiled again.

"Damn! That's great," I exclaimed. "Whereabouts?"

"Naples, originally," Honie told me.

"That's only two, three hours from here."

"She's a lot closer than that," Honie told me, still wearing that somewhat strange smile.

"How do you know?" I wondered.

"Well, I called the contact number on her tour record file," she told me. "Got hold of her parents. They said she's living someplace else these days."

"Where?"

"Right here," Honie said.

"In Miami?"

"You got it."

"I don't suppose you got her address?"

"As a matter of fact, I did," Honie said, smiling at me. She held up a slip of paper.

"Let me guess," I said. "She's an assistant pro at some swanky country club."

"Wrong," Honie Carlton told me. "She's a stripper in a titty bar in Coconut Grove. Place called La Doll House." She gave me the slip of paper which had the address. "She, er, dances interpretatively under the name of 'Tawny.' "

Honie was by now giggling, in part because of the informa-

146

tion she was giving me, in part because of the look on my face. "Well," I said finally, "it's a dirty job, but somebody has to do it." I tucked the address away in my shirt pocket.

"I thought you'd say that." Honie laughed.

CHAPTER 21

Coconut Grove is Miami's yuppie nighttime headquarters. The nightclub district is chockablock with watering holes, elegant restaurants, desserteries, comedy clubs, and other establishments that cater to Miami's young, rich, and elegantly dressed. The Don Johnson and Melanie Griffith wannabees.

The outer fringes of the Grove, however, tend to drift toward the tawdry. Here you'll find the workingmen's bars, with neon beer signs in the windows and music by jukebox. The corners out here are dominated by fast-food joints rather than elegant eateries with chalkboard menus.

La Doll House was one of the fringe joints. A huge garish sign dominated the streetscape. The sign featured a mostly naked woman, from the rear, hip cocked provocatively, arms reaching out tauntingly, long blond hair cascading down her back. THE GROVE'S HOTTEST SHOW, promised the sign. Sounded good to me. I put my rental car in the crowded parking lot and joined the queue waiting to get inside.

The cover charge was ten dollars, collected by a smiling hostess in a shimmery green dress that featured décolletage down to the navel. "Two-drink minimum, boys," she gushed at us. The inside of the place was decorated in mirrored walls, chrome furniture, and lots of flashing lights. There was a main stage of white Plexiglas, lighted underneath, which had twin runways extending out in a V-shape into the center of the place, and thick chrome posts extending upward into the mirrored ceiling. The posts were for the dancers to hang on while they lasciviously bumped and ground. The seats lining these runways were jammed. Twin side stages which featured chrome birdcagelike areas flanked the main stage. There was a naked woman cavorting in each birdcage. A shorter runway extended the length of the back of the place, and more spotlights highlighted the gyrating bodies dancing there. Tables for four were scattered through the interior regions.

The music was cacophonous. Scantily dressed waitresses bustled around taking drink orders. Beer seemed to be the adult beverage of choice in the place. I ordered one. When my waitress brought it to me, she leaned provocatively over and yelled in my ear above the din of the loud music.

"That'll be five bucks," she hollered. I thought about telling her it was against my religion to pay more than three dollars for a beer, but decided that she was too busy to sympathize.

I glanced around La Doll House, after, of course, I had checked out the dancing babes. First things first. The girls were not unfortunate looking and were, I quickly established, quite naked. "Nice deduction," I told myself. Other than that, not interesting in the least. When I finally got around to surveying my surroundings, I noticed that it was a good night: the place was crowded. The all-male audience reflected a cross section of socioeconomic types. As in most strip joints I had visited in my life, there seemed to be three general categories of patrons present.

First was the party crowd. Boys-night-out guys whose membership in the male-bonding group enabled them to act giddy and silly. Which they did with aplomb. They whistled and yelled and motioned for the dancing girls to come near so that they could slip dollar bills into their garter belts. This transaction was accomplished with more catcalls, rolled eyes, flushed foreheads. The naked women seemed to bear the ordeal with patience and forbearance. It was for them, after all, a living. The party boys were slugging down five-dollar beers at a staggering rate, apparently unconcerned with the sacrilege, and the safety of their number made it permissible for them to be openly demonstrative.

Next were the regulars. Guys who probably hung out at La Doll House several times a week. To them it was just a friendly neighborhood tavern, perhaps a bit louder than most, but still a place to hang with the guys, drop a few brews, and, oh yeah, a place to watch women publically flaunt their sexual organs. You could tell the regulars by their studied nonchalance and their general nonattention. They had seen it all before.

Finally, there were the quiet ones, the watchers. These men wore small, self-deprecating smiles, but in their haunted eyes, if you could see them through the colored gloom of the place, you could see pain and desire and the entire range of stunted human sexual emotion. But only in their eyes, which were locked on the gyrating bodies nearby. They otherwise sat quietly, their untouched beer turning warm and flat, their eyes fastened on vulvas and breasts and buttocks that bounced and twirled and flashed. The effect was hypnotic on the quiet ones. From time to time, you could see one of them suddenly break free from the spell for a moment, blink rapidly, glance around sheepishly, rub his eyes almost in disbelief, and then, inevitably, raise his eyes once again to the lurid and irresistible spectacle.

The waitresses hustled, the dancers stripped, the music throbbed. There were two hostesses plying the seats, each dressed in a sequined, sparkling, strapless number that fit like a second skin. Their job was to take orders for table dances. For a special extra fee, usually twenty dollars, a group of men at one of the side tables could special order a girl to come do a custom strip performance at their table. Kind of a private peep show that everybody else got to watch. So I watched a few of the table dancers do their thing. They came out from backstage draped in some kind of naughty Victoria's Secret lingerie. They made a big fuss in meeting all the guys at the table, usually sitting on each one's lap, tickling them under the chin, planting kisses on their ears.

Then, they would teasingly strip, dropping the brassiere slowly down, letting pendulous breasts sway back and forth in rhythm to the beat of the disco music. A leg would go up on the table, and the teddy or the panty would be oh-so-slowly eased down. Most of the time, the girl had the full and rapt attention of her table, and would reap a sizable tip.

I also noticed the bouncer hovering nearby in case some drunken patron might be tempted to touch instead of look. That's a cardinal sin in a titty bar, punishable by instant removal via scruff of the neck. At La Doll House, security seemed to be in the hands of leather-clad biker types. They wore, in addition to glistening black jackets, dark wrap-around sunglasses, silvery earrings, and long hair pulled back in ponytails. The bouncers were very, very large men who no doubt had played the interior line in high school. Just knowing they were there served as an effective deterrent to most of the guys in the bar.

I motioned a hostess over to my table, where I sat alone.

"Hey, fella, feelin' lonely?" she asked, smiling at me after she had slunk over.

"Yeah, kinda," I said. "Is Tawny working tonight?"

"I think she comes on later, like a couple of hours," the hostess told me. "Anyone else you got in mind?"

"Nah, I'd really like to see Tawny," I said, and I slipped her a twenty.

She smiled at me with cold, seen-everything eyes. "Sure, honey," she said. "Have a few drinks. I'll get her when she comes in."

It was more than two hours before Tawny got there. In the long, long interval while I waited, I did what everyone else in La Doll House was doing: watched the girls. I saw all the body types as they came out to perform: the huge big-breasted types, the skinny, barely-anything-there types, and most every variation in between. Some of the girls ran to chubby, some had been to the plastic surgeon for a little augmentation, but others had hard, lithe bodies that showed off a lot of physical work in the gym. Some were butt-ugly, some were rather pretty. Most had hard, tired, and cold eyes.

They all were smiling, because it was their job to smile. When they had finished stripping, and were standing on the stage naked, clinging to the chrome bars, they all tried to make their faces look pouty, in a kind of mock-sexy look, subgenus *Playboy*. Sometimes I saw faked passion, sometimes plastic seductiveness.

But it was their eyes that always betrayed them. Their eyes said that they knew they were appealing to human depravity and that they didn't like it one bit . . . *hated* it, in fact . . . but a girl has to earn a living, so what the hell, go ahead and look, you pigs, you absolute low-life disgusting pigs.

The bodies aroused, while the eyes depressed. I tried to modulate both emotions with a half-dozen beers. I was largely unsuccessful in that effort, and was thinking about upgrading to Scotch, when a soft hand tapped me on the shoulder, and I turned to face Tawny, née Cindy D'Angelo, professional golfer.

She was a striking woman, on the tall side, with straight blond hair that hung down to frame her face. It was something of a throwback to the late sixties, the Marianne Faithful look. The blond went dark at the roots. She wore a purple teddy number with pearl snaps down the front, and her front was substantial. Her breasts strained against the material, and her nipples made two soft dents. The teddy thing flared out just below her waist, barely covering what looked like a matching thong bikini. Her figure was trim, but I could see that it had once been an athletic form. Her legs were still strong and muscular, and betrayed the soft baby-doll look she was striving for. Her eyes were dark and cold, like the other girls', and heavily mascara-ed. She had also applied purple streaks around her cheekbones, which gave her face a garish look— hard, yet exotic.

"I understand you've got a special request," Tawny breathed at me, and reaching down, she grabbed my earlobe between her teeth and gave it a nip while breathing lustfully into my ear.

"I sure do," I breathed back, trying to look overcome. "I want to spend a few minutes talking with Cindy D'Angelo, girl golfer."

She straining up, her eyes narrowing sharply, her lips pursed into a sudden frown. She looked at me appraisingly.

"You don't look like a cop," she said.

"Nope," I said. "Worse. Writer."

She blew out a breath that sounded like "Pfaw" and looked away. She put a hand on her hip and turned to stare at me.

"I don't do interviews," she said.

"It's not an interview," I told her. "I just need some background information." She looked dubious. "Really," I pleaded. "I just need five minutes. Your name will never hit print. Please?"

My mother was right. Manners are important. Tawny blew out another breath, this time in resignation, and motioned me to follow her as she headed toward the back of the bar. On the way down the crowded aisle, one of the beefy leather boys intercepted her. She whispered a few quick words in his ear and he stood out of the way. I guess he might have been glaring at me as I passed, but his reflective dark glasses prevented me from seeing his eyes. It felt like a glare, anyway.

She led me down past the main stage and through a thick curtain beside it. A short hallway led to a large open area behind the main stage, where the girls not dancing were repairing makeup and hair in front of a large, mirrored wall. Most of them were nude. I tried not to look. And failed.

"Okay, man," Tawny said to me. "Five minutes. And it'll cost you twenty. My time is valuable, y'know." She glared at me, suspicious.

"Where'd you get the neat name?" I asked her as I slipped her a bill.

She rolled her eyes. At least it wasn't a question she was expecting. "My manager," she said. "And I suppose you want to know how a girl went from the wholesome fairways of the professional golf tour to being a stripper. Well, I make a whole lot more money doing this with a whole lot less effort. So to answer your question—"

153

"I didn't ask," I said quietly.

She stared at me for a moment, then smiled. It was a pretty smile, underneath all that long straight blond hair.

"Sorry," she said. "Soapbox time. What's your name, anyway?"

I held out my hand, and she took it. "Hacker," I said. "I write golf for the *Boston Journal.*"

She smiled at me. "Where'd you get the neat name?"

We laughed together, the ice finally broken. "So," I said, "how does a nice girl go from the wholesome fairways . . ."

She laughed again. "Say," she said, "do you think you can get me a couple of passes for the tournament this weekend? I haven't seen the girls play for a few years now."

"Sure thing," I told her. "Do you want them left under Cindy or Tawny?"

"Cindy's fine." She smiled. "So what can I do for you, Hacker?"

"I don't know if you heard, but Benton Bergmeister died yesterday," I told her. I watched her face for reaction. Did her eyes widen fractionally? I couldn't tell for sure. I guessed that years of practice in disguising her emotions in a place like La Doll House came in handy.

"Oh, that's too bad," she said politely and noncommittedly. "He was a nice old guy."

"Yeah, I thought so, too," I said. "Anyway, I'm here because there is a rumor that Benton had some deep dark secret in his past, and that same rumor says you are it."

"I see," she said. Her eyes had narrowed and turned to ice.

"So, I thought I'd come track you down and let you comment on those rumors. You can deny everything, of course, and I'll go away and leave you alone. Or, you can help me out and tell me what happened."

"And what's in it for me, Hacker?" she snapped, eyes flashing angrily.

I held out my hands and shrugged. "Nothing that I can think of," I told her honestly. "Maybe a little peace of mind, putting to rest something that might still be troubling?" I stopped, it sounded lame even to me.

Tawny chewed on her lower lip and stared off into space for a long moment. Finally, she turned and looked at me.

"Hell, if the guy's dead, I guess it doesn't matter anymore, does it?" She leaned back against the wall, closed her eyes, and began to talk.

"I turned pro when I was seventeen," she began. "I know now that was way too soon, but I thought I had the world by the short hairs. I was all-everything in Florida, beating everybody, girls my age and even most of the college players. I even trimmed Kathy Whitworth in an exhibition match when I was sixteen. I found out later that she had the flu that day. That year I was a semifinalist in the U.S. Amateur. Youngest ever. Everybody said I was a 'can't miss,' and I believed all my press clippings."

She opened her eyes and smiled at me, then leaned back and closed them once again.

"So I came out on tour. It was either that or go to college for four years, and I decided making money was a better idea. 'The Florida Schoolgirl,' they called me. It was good PR for the tour. But I was far too young. Naive. Innocent. Hadn't finished growing yet, but I thought that didn't matter. Thought I would continue to win easily, and I didn't. Hell, I lost everything. Couldn't drive, couldn't hit irons, four-putted greens . . . everything. After three horrible tournaments in a row, I was ready to pack it in and come home.

"That's when Benton stepped in and took over. He saw what was happening and tried to help. Isolated me from the press, assigned another player to stay with me on the road, tried to spend time just talking with me whenever he could. He'd try to have dinner with me a few times each week when he was around."

She opened her eyes and looked at me again. This time her eyes were wet.

"He was really being nice," she told me. "And his program was working. I calmed down and had a few good tournaments in a row, started to get some confidence back. Then, one night, he jumped me."

"Jumped you?" I asked.

155

"He'd been drinking, before, during, and after dinner that night," Tawny continued. "He was walking me back to my hotel room, when he suddenly turned and pounced. Drunken kisses, hands everywhere, ripping my clothes. It was pretty awful."

"How'd you escape?" I asked. "A swift kick to the co-jones?"

She laughed. "Naw, I told you, I was just an innocent schoolgirl. I didn't even know what was going on. It was just luck that Big Wyn happened down the hotel path that night, and she stopped him."

"Wynnona Stilwell," I said, and sighed heavily.

"Yeah," Tawny nodded. "Lucky for me, I guess, unlucky for Benton. She was really breathing fire at him when she pulled him off. He immediately went all contrite and started blubbering. God, what a scene." She shook her head in remembrance.

"What happened next?" I asked.

"Well," Tawny said, "the next day, Big Wyn came to see me, with a lawyer in tow. She had some papers for me to sign. She explained that they were agreements not to sue Benton or the Tour, and told me that if I signed, she'd take care of me."

"Take care . . . ?" I let the question hang.

"She meant extra bennies," Tawny explained. "Good rooms, good tee times, upgrades to first-class airline tickets, stuff like that. In return, I was supposed to agree not to sue Benton Bergmeister or the LPGA Tour for what he had done to me. Hell, I never even thought about doing something like that. I just wanted to forget the whole thing and go play some golf. So I signed both papers."

"Both papers?" I queried.

Tawny smiled at me approvingly. "You're quick, Hacker. I'll give you that," she said. "Yeah, two papers. I remember glancing at the first one, and reading some of the legal mumbo jumbo. It was about what Big Wyn told me. So I signed it, and the paper under it, just like the lawyer guy told me. It was a couple of years later that I learned the second document I signed wasn't just a copy of the first. Friend of mine on the players' committee had seen it."

"What was it?" I wondered.

"Basically, a declaration that I was planning to press charges against Benton Bergmeister for attempted rape, sexual abuse, and transporting a minor across state lines for immoral purposes . . . minor stuff like that." She smiled at me, grim and humorless.

"But you said you didn't want to press charges, just forget the whole episode," I said.

"Exactly," Tawny said. "But Big Wyn and her lawyer got me to sign that second paper without looking at it. And once they had it signed and notarized, they had Benton Bergmeister's balls in their pocket.

"Big Wyn showed it to Benton and told him I was real anxious to prosecute him for rape and that he was looking at some hard time in the slammer, but that she had been able to convince me to hold off on pressing charges. And that as long as he did what she wanted, she would continue to protect his sorry ass from the police and the publicity. And if he didn't . . ."

"I'd have called her bluff," I said.

Tawny smiled at me.

"You men are so macho," she said. "Benton did call her bluff. At least, that's what I heard later in locker room gossip. He supposedly told her she couldn't do that to him."

"What did Big Wyn do?"

Tawny smiled again, this time without pleasure.

"She sent a copy of my signed and rather lurid statement to Benton's wife."

"Jeezus."

"Who immediately filed divorce proceedings, got a large settlement, and turned Benton's little girl against him." Tawny looked at me again, clear-eyed and cold. "Benton wasn't so macho after that," she said. "In fact, it was right about then that he started drinking a lot."

I thought about Big Wyn's strange and triumphant look when Bergmeister's family had come up in the press room

157

after his death. Now I knew why she had looked victorious: She had beaten this man, definitively and decisively, destroyed his life, damaged his family. Pretty good day's work.

"And you didn't know about any of this at the time?" I asked.

Tawny shook her head side to side. "Nah," she said. "I went back to playing golf, but I never got over the hump. Had some fun, made some friends, struggled like mad, never made much money, and after three years, I quit." She stared off in the distance again as three naked dancers swept past us toward the dressing room.

"Part of it was that I missed what Benton had given me . . . some confidence in myself, some peace of mind. But I kinda burned out on a lot of things at once," she told me finally. "Knocked around for a year or two doing not much at all. Waitress. Boat rat. Didn't even pick up a golf club. My parents finally threw me out. Eventually, I ended up here."

She turned to look at me, her eyes large and sad. "It's pretty good money," she shrugged. "But I miss golf. And the Tour. I had some really good friends." She sighed, once, deeply.

"Did you get all the perks Big Wyn promised?" I asked.

"Yeah, she took pretty good care of me," Tawny said. "No complaints."

"She come on to you?"

Tawny looked at me with a strange smile.

"Hacker, you've got a dirty mind," she said, laughing softly. "Or, you've been talking out of school to somebody. To answer your question, not really. She let it be known that she was available, but I was just a kid and really hadn't gotten into sex. But I knew about Big Wyn and the others, who they were and all. You learn these things pretty quickly . . . who's who and what's what . . . and just go on playing golf."

I looked at the girl for a minute, turning something over in my mind.

"Listen, Cindy," I said. "I know I said I just needed some background, but it would help if you'd agree to go public with this."

She was shaking her head.

"No way, man," she said. "I don't want to become a public figure, a tabloid queen, or go on Phil Donahue's show. It might be hard for someone like you to understand, but this is a pretty good job. Doesn't involve any heavy lifting, I like the hours, and the money's good . . . damn good. I'm not about to rock the boat by becoming your star witness. No way."

"Look," I said. "Benton's dead. I still don't know exactly how or why, but he's assumed room temperature, and I believe Big Wyn is behind it, somehow or other. The woman has ruined a bunch of lives and careers, but Benton is dead. I think it's time someone said stop. I can start the ball rolling, but I gotta have a source. You're it. You're the hold she had on Benton. You're the thing that might have caused that poor, drunken man to decide death was better than fighting Big Wyn. Think about it. He gave up. I'm not going to. I need your help."

She was chewing her bottom lip nervously as I gave her my best freedom-of-the-press sermon. Hold high the banner of truth, and all that.

I think it was working, but just at that moment, a huge sunburned man in a sleeveless T-shirt and dirty blue jeans staggered through the curtained doorway from the main bar. His face was shaggy with several days' growth of beard, his eyes narrow and unfocused. He had a large gut, flabby arms, and brown leather cowboy boots.

"Omigod," he gasped, staring at Tawny in her purple teddy. "Honeybunch, you an' me got some serious dancin' to do. C'mere!"

He lurched forward, his big beefy hands reaching up to grasp her breasts. Squeezing and pulling, his hands tore open the pearl snaps on her teddy. It happened so fast she didn't have time to react defensively. I heard her squeal in furious dismay.

"Hey!" I yelled and started toward the drunken brute. I didn't have time for much more. Out of the corner of my eye I saw a black flash, which mobilized in front of me as one of the leather-clad rogue bouncers. He was moving, and moving fast.

The bouncer smashed one beefy forearm across the drunken guy's neck, a tremendous blow which resulted in a pained grunt from the drunk. His head and his shoulders came up in surprise. That gave Tawny an opening to step back and send a knee flying upward to the man's groin. That got a groan. By then, the bouncer had a full nelson on the guy and slammed his face into the wall. That put his lights out.

I turned to see if Tawny was okay, but it was only a half-turn. In the next second, my arm had been twisted up high behind my back, right to the breaking point, and my face was suddenly studying closely the paint job of the wall on the other side of the hallway.

"Go ahead, scumbag," hissed a voice at my ear. "Resist a little. I haven't broken an arm in months."

"Rocky, ease off, man," I heard Tawny protest. "It wasn't him. We was just talkin'."

Reluctantly, Rocky let go of my arm, which I painfully unfolded and flexed a few times to make sure it still worked. I turned around. The drunk was on the floor, snoring peacefully through a bloody face. He appeared to be missing a few of his teeth. Rocky and an equally fearful-looking compatriot stood there looking fierce. Tawny was examining her breasts and wincing.

"Goddamn," she said as she fingered each one unself-consciously. "Son of a bitch grabbed so hard he left bruises. Shit!"

"Baby! Are you okay?" wailed a soft feminine voice. One of the other dancers ran up to Tawny. She had lots of curly red hair piled atop her head, but in the bright, harsh light, I could see dark roots beneath. I also noted the beginnings of wrinklets gathering under her eyes and around her neck. Her body, wrapped in a short terry robe, looked good at first glance, but in the thighs I could see the beginnings of heaviness. The redhead was obviously a veteran of the nude-dancing wars.

"What's happened, baby? Are you okay? Do you need to see a doctor?" the redhead gushed at Tawny and she pulled her into a protective embrace. She turned to face the bouncers. "Goddamnit! Where were you guys? You're supposed to stop stuff like this! She coulda been hurt!"

160

"It's okay, Doris, relax," Tawny said. "I'm fine. Just a damn drunk with frisky hands. I may be wearing his fingerprints on my tits, that's all."

"Oh, baby, how awful!" gushed Doris. "You come back here with me right now and let me look. I'll kiss 'em and make 'em better, baby, you know I can!"

Doris slipped her arm around Tawny's waist and started to lead her away.

"Cindy?"

I threw my hands out in appeal.

She looked back at me once.

"Okay, Hacker," she said. "For Benton's sake. Okay."

"I'll leave you some tickets," I called. "Thanks."

Tawny nodded, then turned to go with the redhead. I saw her rest her head gently on the other woman's shoulder and slip her arm lovingly around Doris's waist as they disappeared in the back.

The two bouncers watched the women go. "Shit," one growled. The other bent over, grabbed the snoring, bloody drunk by the belt and scruff of the neck, and effortlessly hauled him out the door.

The other one glared wordlessly at me, so I left, under my own power.

161

CHAPTER 22

When I got back to the hotel about half past nine, the message light on my phone was blinking. I called the operator and she told me that Don Collier had called. I dialed the security office.

"Ah, Hacker," he said. "Where you been?"

"Sampling some of Miami's most elegant nightlife," I told him.

"Well, there have been all sorts of interesting new developments," he told me.

The autopsy had been performed that afternoon. The docs had found that Benton Bergmeister's blood alcohol level was right through the roof. He had apparently drunk most of that bottle of Scotch found by his bedside table in his room.

But that hadn't killed him . . . not directly. It was the Nembutal interacting with all that booze that had done him in.

"Nembutal?" I asked. "Isn't that like a sleeping pill or something?"

"Yeah, a depressant," Collier said. "Used as a sedative. Not good to mix with alcohol. It'll kill ya."

I thought for a minute.

"But Bergmeister must have known that," I protested. "He wasn't stupid. So that means he either killed himself, or, drunk, he just accidentally swallowed the wrong pills."

"Well, there's more to it than that," Collier said. "I went back and checked my inventory . . . you know, the list I made while I was trying not to stare down that woman's dress?"

"And?"

"And none of the medications she packed up was Nembutal," Collier said. "According to my list, the guy didn't have any."

"What was he taking?"

"According to my list, there were some antibiotics, some antacids, and something called Minizide, which the label on the bottle said was for blood pressure."

"And none of those contained Nembutal?"

"Nope."

"And wouldn't cause a similar kind of reaction with booze?"

"Not according to the doc at the morgue I talked with," Collier said. "But the lab will do a complete analysis as soon as the pills show up."

"Where are they?"

Collier sighed. "Well, the bombshell had already shipped the boxes of his personal effects out to Bergmeister's daughter out in California, pills included. So we have to wait for them to arrive out there, and then get them back down here. Probably take a week or two."

"Damn," I said. I hate unanswered questions. Then I thought of something.

"Couple of days ago, Benton mentioned that he needed to have a prescription refilled," I told Collier. "If he did, there's got to be a record of it somewhere that can be checked—make sure he got the right stuff."

"Shit, Hacker," Collier groaned. "There's gotta be a thousand pharmacies in greater Miami. You want me to tell the cops to start calling each one?"

"Isn't there one that the hotel recommends?" I asked. "If a

163

guest comes looking for a drugstore? Chances are, that's where he got his refilled."

"Hmmm. Not bad, Hacker. I'll check into it." Collier rang off.

I sat in my room for a while, thinking, turning ideas over in my head. Finally, I decided it was time to do something tangible and concrete.

First, I got on the phone and called the Dade County Medical Examiner's Office. About ten phone calls later, I got the basic information Collier had given me confirmed. Death was from the reaction between booze and Nembutal. Bergmeister's case had been reopened pending further investigation.

Once I had my sources and information verified, I opened my trusty Compaq laptop and began to write. It started out as a Pulitzer Prize winner.

> Benton T. Bergmeister, the commissioner of the Ladies' Professional Golf Tour who died suddenly yesterday in Miami, had been blackmailed for more than ten years by one of the Tour's most famous players, the *Boston Journal* has learned.
>
> In a stunning revelation, sources indicated that allegations of sexual misconduct had been used against Bergmeister to ensure his continued allegiance and support for the policies of Wynnona Stilwell, the president of the LPGA Players' Committee and one of the most accomplished women in the history of golf.
>
> The story was revealed by Cindy D'Angelo, a former golfer on the LPGA Tour, who was the victim of an alleged sexual attack by Bergmeister. Ms. D'Angelo, who is now a dancer in a Miami nightclub, said she was duped by LPGA officials into signing a document which was subsequently used to blackmail the commissioner to ensure his cooperation.
>
> Bergmeister died suddenly Thursday in his hotel room in Miami, where the LPGA is staging the Miami Classic golf tournament this weekend.
>
> The circumstances surrounding his death have yet to be

164

officially revealed, but the *Journal* has learned that an unusual change in Bergmeister's medication may be responsible for his death.

According to results of an autopsy performed on Bergmeister's body yesterday, his death was attributed to a fatal combination of alcohol and the drug Nembutal, a barbiturate.

While Bergmeister was known as a heavy drinker, investigators in Miami are trying to trace the source of the Nembutal, a medication not among many prescribed for the late commissioner. Police do not know how Bergmeister got the Nembutal or why he took it.

Sources within the LPGA have painted a picture of that organization as being under the firm control of Mrs. Stilwell, who has been a member of the professional golfing organization since 1965 and president of its policy-making players' committee for the last thirteen years.

My story continued for several more graphs, until the point where I knew I'd have to insert a protesting note of innocence from Big Wyn. I glanced at my watch and decided it was too late to call her tonight for the quote. Since all hell would no doubt break loose when I talked to her, I wasn't unhappy about waiting one more day. I reread what I'd written, trying to anticipate what objections my gun-shy editor would raise. He'd once been a helluva reporter, but when they move upstairs, plop their ever-widening butts into those creaky wooden chairs, and become high and mighty, they suddenly lose nine-tenths of their guts. Every other word out of their mouth is either "liability" or "verifiable."

I was still at work a few minutes later when I was startled by a loud rapping at my door. I looked at my watch again: just shy of midnight.

When I opened it, a waiter in a starched white coat stood in the hall, a heavily laden trolley in front of him.

"Room service," he said, smiling.

"You must have the wrong room," I protested. "I didn't order anything from room service."

165

"No, but I think you asked a girl out to dinner," said a female voice, and Sybil Montgomery stepped into view.

I slapped my forehead. "I forgot," I said.

"Well, I didn't," she said smartly and pushed me aside. "Come then, dearie. Let the man work. I am utterly famished."

Sybil plopped down in a chair while the smiling waiter laid out the meal. She had ordered two steaks, salad, baked potatoes, and a bottle of red wine. It smelled heavenly as the waiter popped the silver tops off the plates. It occurred to me that I had eaten nothing all day but had consumed a rather vast quantity of beer, both with Harold Stilwell and at La Doll House. I was hungry, too.

"You are amazing," I told her.

"Not at all." She smiled back at me. "I just know how to take care of myself. No sense waiting around for other people to do or not do what one can very well do for herself."

"How'd you play today?"

"Not awful," she said, waving a hand in dismissal. "Two under. I should think two more rounds the same would do very nicely."

"I should think rather," I tweaked.

The waiter finished unpacking and made to leave.

"No ticket?" I asked him. He smiled and told me the lady had taken care of it. Sybil smiled enigmatically at me. I gave the guy a couple of dollars, and he bowed out of the room.

As I opened the wine, I looked at Sybil and the dinner.

"You do seem to know how to take care of yourself," I said.

"Quite," she said.

"And you appear to get what you want," I mused aloud. "Up to and including, it seems, me."

"What I want right now is dinner," she said, evading my eyes. She took up her knife and fork and cut a piece of beef.

"And after?"

Her chin came out defensively. "Sex," she said defiantly, her eyes flashing at me now, "is one of the primary human drives. I do not apologize for that, nor do I feel it necessary to have to explain myself."

"No," I countered, "you don't have to explain yourself, which is something you don't seem to want to do. You just pop in and pop out whenever you feel like it."

She threw down her utensils and stood up. Her face was a splotchy red.

"Do you wish me to leave, Hacker?" she demanded.

"No, Sybil, I want you to stay," I said quietly. "I just want to get to know the real you, the inside you. Not just the bloody human drives you've got."

Our eyes locked across the table and its steaming steaks. Slowly, Sybil sank back down. Silently, I poured the wine. She took hers, sipped, replaced the glass, and sighed.

"I'm sorry, Hacker," she said. "You are right. I am not used to opening up very much. This is such a nomadic existence most of the time, one learns not to dare. The people one tends to meet are either horrible users or they're gone in a week's time."

"Like I will be," I said.

She sighed again. "Yes, dammit, like you will be." She looked up at me, her eyes suddenly wet. "But I feel something different with you," she said. "Don't ask me why. Just a feeling that says there's something special about you. That's a scary feeling for me to have, much less admit."

I leaned over the table and clinked her wine glass with mine.

"Well, here's to scary feelings," I said. "And here's to that wonderful, something-special feeling that goes with it. Because I have it, too. So even though you'll be heading west and I north come Monday, I think it's a safe bet that our paths will be crossing again soon. Because I don't get that feeling much, either."

She reached over and squeezed my hand. We neither had to speak, because we both felt it and understood and were glad.

"What have you discovered about that Cindy person?" she asked after a time.

I reached over for my laptop, handed it to her, and showed her how to work the arrow keys to scroll the copy. While she read, I attacked my steak.

167

She finished, sat back in her chair, and looked at me thoughtfully, lips pursed.

"Will they run this?" she asked.

"I think so."

"The feathers will fly," she said.

"I know."

"I'm not sure the tour will survive," she said. "Sponsors will no doubt drop out. Everyone's sex life will become front-page reading. The networks will probably cancel our already-pitiful schedule. Hacker, do you really think this is wise?"

I stared across the table at her for a moment.

"Don't you think it's time somebody got Big Wyn's jack-boot off your necks?" I asked her. "Isn't it time for someone to step forward and say enough is enough? Besides, what do you care if the LPGA falls apart? You can just trip off back home to England and ignore the whole mess."

"I suppose I deserved that," Sybil said, but I could tell I'd hurt her feelings.

"I'm sorry, lady," I apologized. "That was low. Listen, I didn't ask to be the one to blow the whistle. But somebody would do it sooner or later, and besides, it's my job. But it's up to someone else to take control of this organization and make it work the way it's supposed to. I don't give a rat's ass if it's you, or Mary Beth Burke or Nancy Lopez or Josephine the Cat. All I know is that Wynnona Stilwell's reign as queen is over."

She studied me. "I do hope you're right," she murmured.

CHAPTER 23

I awoke early and lay quietly thinking while the rising sun filled the room with soft light. After a time, I leaned over and kissed awake the sleeping form beside me. Sybil stirred, moaned softly, and finally opened her eyes.

"Sixty-nine," I said.

"Dear me," she said. "I don't know you quite that well, do I? And besides, I fear we're both a mite sticky from last night, aren't we, darling?"

To prove her point, she reached down beneath the sheet and stroked me. She was right. Still sticky.

I laughed. "No, you boob, I just had an intuitive flash that you're going to shoot sixty-nine today. That number came into my head and stayed there."

"Ah, I see," Sybil said, and actually blushed. I kissed her some more. "In that case, will you just phone the score in for me? I'd like a few more hours of sleep."

"C'mon," I said, throwing back the sheets. "Up and at 'em. We've got worlds to conquer."

I ordered breakfast to be sent to the room. We washed off

each other's sticky parts in a steamy shower and threw on the hotel's comfortable terry robes. We shared breakfast and the morning paper on the small balcony.

"I believe I'll need all of that sixty-nine today," Sybil murmured as she read the sports page. "Beth Daniel did a sixty-six yesterday, and she's been playing extremely well of late. Ah, well, off to the wars."

She rose, dressed, and, before leaving, came back out on the balcony for a farewell kiss.

"Do be careful, Hacker, dear," she murmured against my cheek. "The Queen is not yet dead, and I fear she has a few poisoned apples up her sleeve."

"Thanks for the warning." I laughed. "But I've got truth, justice, and the American way on my side."

She kissed me again, looked deeply into my eyes, and left.

When I made it to the pressroom an hour later, I sat down and penned a quick note. Sealing it in an envelope, I sought out Honie Carlton, who was busy entering first-round statistics into a computer terminal.

"Hey, Hacker," she greeted me, sitting back from the drudge work with a sigh. "How did the search go last night?"

"Illuminating and eye-opening," I said with a straight face. She laughed aloud.

"Do you know what Big Wyn's schedule is today?" I asked.

"I think she had an early tee time today," Honie said, reaching for a pairings sheet on the table in front of her. "Yeah, they went off an hour ago, so she should be finished right after lunch. Whaddya need?"

"I want you to tell her I need an interview with her ASAP," I said. "Private and one-on-one. And give her this." I handed her the sealed envelope.

"What is it?" Honie asked.

"Incentive," I said mysteriously, and left.

I had time to kill, so I went out on the course to watch some golf. I caught up with Betsy King's threesome on the front nine. King has been near the top of the women's money list for some years. I watched her play a few shots. Smooth, steady swing, classically correct, but mechanical-looking. On the golf course, she is all business. She pulls her visor down low over her eyes, and you can feel her uninterrupted concentration. All her movements are deliberate, calm, unemotional. It's like watching a golfing machine at work: bloodless, cold, yet terribly efficient. She made a birdie at eight to pull within one of the leaders.

Bored, I wandered away through the crowds. Cutting back over to the back side, I came upon Patty Sheehan's group. Looking at the scoreboard carried by a young volunteer, I saw that Patty wasn't having a good tournament: She had fallen to one under par, eight shots behind.

But watching her play, you couldn't tell. Patty plays a game diametrically opposed to Betsy King. She wears her heart on her sleeve, for all to see. Where Betsy King walks deliberately and slowly from tee to her ball, head still, eyes straight ahead, saying nothing, and acknowledging no one, Patty Sheehan practically dances down a fairway. I watched her hit a pulled drive that flew straight, but down the left side, ending up in the rough, and for the first forty steps down the fairway, Sheehan pulled her visor off and slapped her thigh with it with every step as if in self-punishment. Then she grinned to herself, popped the visor back on, looked over at the fans along the ropes, waved to a friend, slapped her caddy on the back, and strode on to her ball. I followed.

Her ball was sitting up in the rough, which was lucky, but the fairway bent away to the left, and three tall sabal palms blocked her view of the green. She stood behind her ball for a moment, studying the options. Her caddy whispered the yardage to her, and she nodded and pulled a club out of the bag. While she waited for a playing partner to make her shot across the fairway, she looked over at the gallery ropes and saw me standing there.

"Watch this, Hacker," she called. "Piece of cake."

She took a couple of practice swings, then stepped up to the ball. She had taken a long iron—it looked like a three—which was a dangerous club to play in that thick rough. A three-iron doesn't have much loft, and anything less than precise contact could cause the club to get hung up in the thick grass, further closing the face and leading to an ugly shanked result. But she made a typical Sheehan swing—smooth, rhythmic—and caught the ball cleanly.

It shot off down the right center of the fairway, low and hot, then began hooking sharply, curving perfectly to the left around the trees and the corner. Straining, I saw the ball land in the fairway about thirty yards short of the green. Because of its hook overspin, the ball began to run. I saw it punch through the collar of bermuda rough around the green, and then I lost sight of it.

But the crowd around the green watched, and roared in waves of enthusiastic approval, as the ball continued to trickle down the green, closer and closer to the hole.

Patty couldn't see where the ball finished, either, but we could both tell from the cheers echoing down the fairway that her miracle shot had finished close to the hole.

She looked over at me with a huge ear-to-ear grin on her face. I gave her a thumbs-up. She threw her hands up in the air and waggled her legs back and forth in an excellent imitation of an NFL halfback celebrating a touchdown. The fans around me laughed and cheered wildly.

Back in the pressroom, an hour or so later, I got word that Big Wyn would give me half an hour at four. That message was relayed to me by Karla, the Tour's PR honcho and Honie's boss. I had not seen Honie Carlton since she left the pressroom with my message. Karla sought me out shortly after lunch. She wore a conservative gray business suit with a colorful print scarf on the shoulder and a diamond-encrusted lapel pin in the shape of a flagstick.

"May I ask the purpose of your interview with Mrs. Stilwell?" she asked me earnestly.

"You certainly may," I said. "But I won't tell you. It's between Wyn and me."

She didn't like that, but there wasn't anything she could do

172

about it. I put my face back into the newspaper I had been reading and propped my feet up on the desk.

That's probably why she gave me the cold-shoulder treatment when she came to escort me up to Big Wyn's suite a few minutes before four. I was going to ask her if she liked being a high-paid escort, but I figured she might take my question the wrong way, so I shut up. She was stonily silent, so I settled for whistling tunelessly as the private elevator whisked us up.

When the door opened, I told Karla I could find my own way, and she stayed in the elevator as the doors closed with a whisper. I walked past the smoky mirrors, down the curving hall, and out to the dramatic balcony overlooking the living room. Down below, Big Wyn sat quietly by herself in the plush white leather sofa. She was looking at a scrap of paper I recognized as the note I had sent earlier with Honie. I walked down the staircase and sat down in a chair next to the sofa.

She didn't look at me. Big Wyn looked tired. She had, I knew, just completed eighteen holes of tournament golf, but this was more than that. Her eyes were wrinkled at the corners. Her face was etched with fatigue, and her shoulders seemed to sag. This was not the confident, triumphant Wynnona Stilwell, conqueror of the fairways. This was a tired, aging, and somewhat apprehensive old woman.

"So, who's Cindy D'Angelo?" Big Wyn rasped at me when I sat down, brandishing the notepaper she held in her hand. "Somebody I'm supposed to know?"

I looked at her for a moment.

"That's good, Wyn," I said. "Denial. But it won't work. I've talked to the girl. I've got the story. It's a good one, too."

"C'mon, Hacker," she laughed, shaking her head. "Who's gonna believe some cockamamy story from a nude dancer . . . a hooker probably?" She looked at me and shook her head. "It'll go down as the ramblings of some cheap little bimbo tryin' to extort some bucks. Who's gonna listen to—"

She broke off abruptly and looked down at her hands. Then she got up and shuffled over to the big floor-to-ceiling window wall which looked out over the golf courses and the crowds of spectators milling about. She stared out the window, her gray-

173

streaked hair suddenly bright with the golden rays of the afternoon sun.

"You don't understand, do you Hacker?" she said softly. "I have worked my entire life for the girls on this Tour. I've worked like hell to get the money up, so we can make a living. Oh, all these smiling sponsors, they'd love to have the women pros play, yes, sir. Love to have those purty gals come to town and perform like trained seals. But when it came time to write the checks, it was, 'We're not gonna pay big money for a bunch of damn pussies!' Oh, Hacker, you don't know the fights I had to go through. In public, when the cameras come on, we're great athletes, fine people, the world's best golfers. But in the back room, when the dollars are on the table, we're bitches, dykes, cunts, you name it. I've been called every name in the book."

She continued to stare out the window. She ran a hand through her straggly hair.

"Until I came along, these girls played for peanuts . . . for nothin'! Did it gladly, too, just because they loved the game! Well, I said the hell with that! I've had to fight to get the purses up. I've had to fight to get television coverage. I've had to fight to get everything. The PGA Tour . . . they just throw money at those sons-a-bitches. But I've had to fight tooth and nail for everything we've got on this Tour. You just don't know . . ."

"I do know, Wyn," I said softly. "I know it's been tough and I know you've done a hell of a job. But you've become part of the problem, not the solution. And you haven't always played fair."

"Fair!" She wheeled to face me, her eyes suddenly afire. "Fair? You think it's fair when the chairman of a major New York bank says he'll sponsor a tournament if I give him a blowjob? You think it's fair when one of my girls wins six tournaments in a year and doesn't get the first kind of commercial endorsement offer? Fair? You think it's fair that it costs us just as much in expenses for being on Tour as men, but that we play for one-third the money? Fair? Don't talk to me about fair, Hacker. There's nothing fair in this life. Fair is what you can make for yourself."

174

"Ah," I said. "The old 'ends justify the means' argument, eh?"

"You are goddamn right," Big Wyn retorted, her face reddening. "I learned pretty damn quick that in this life you got two choices. You either get the other guy, or he gets you. There's no in-between. And I made up my mind early on that I was going to do the getting. Nobody was gonna get the better of Wynnona Haybrook. Nobody."

I studied her for a moment. That defiant chin was jutting out, those fierce eyes sparkling. Big Wyn had put the chip squarely on her shoulder and was just daring someone to knock it off.

There was a germ of truth in Big Wyn's impassioned claim. Women had it tough—women golfers trying to earn a living at their trade were at a comparative disadvantage. It wasn't fair, it wasn't right, but it was the way things were. And Big Wyn deserved credit for the efforts she had made to level the playing field for herself and the other women golfers she represented.

But she had gone beyond the boundary. She had, in effect, made up the rules as she went along. She had kicked the ball out of the bunker, conceded herself long putts, not counted all the strokes. In so doing, she had not merely "cheated," she had broken a trust. Whether for good or ill, the rules exist for a reason, and cannot be ignored at will. At least, not without some consequence. In Big Wyn's case, no one would sign her scorecard.

"Wyn, I've gotta run this," I said. I pulled a copy of my story from my pocket, unfolded it, and handed it to her. "I understand what you're saying, but I've got a responsibility to run it. I'll include any comment you want to make."

Silently, she took the papers and read them. She stopped only once, about halfway through, to look at me with sad eyes, weary once again.

When she finished, she handed me back the sheets of paper and stared out the window into the sunset.

"Comment?" I asked.

She mumbled something.

"I'm sorry?" I said.

175

"Mumbo jumbo," she said. "Bunch a damn mumbo jumbo."

"That your comment?"

She waved her hand in dismissal. "We'll get back with you," she said. "Gotta think."

"Okay," I said. "But I'm sending this up to Boston in an hour. They'll want some reaction from you."

She waved me away again and I left Big Wyn standing at the window in the afternoon sun, standing in the wreckage of her life.

CHAPTER 24

I went back to the pressroom. The day's scores were being tallied and analyzed. I noted that Sybil Montgomery had fired a nifty sixty-eight, putting her two shots out of the lead. I figured I'd call for a congratulatory drink after I had filed my piece.

She had already been brought into the pressroom for the usual after-the-round interview session. Professional golf is probably the only sport in which the reporters covering the event can sit there and have the players brought to them. Requests are placed through the tournament staff to fetch the players who have turned in particularly good rounds, or those in or near the lead. The players come down from the locker room, sit on a dais holding a microphone, and talk about their round, often ending with a hole-by-hole, shot-by-shot description of club and distance. After that, we ask questions.

"So, how do you feel for tomorrow's round?"

"Well, I'll just play them one hole at a time."

Zzzzzzz.

One of these days, before I retire, just for the hell of it I'm gonna ask someone a doozy, like, "In Tolstoy's *War and Peace,* do you think Natasha represents the essential Russian mind?" Just to see what happens.

I waited while the room slowly emptied, the day's work done. Barley Raney was reading *USA Today* in one corner of the room, while a half-dozen volunteer ladies in matching pink golf shirts bustled about, closing up shop for the day.

"Has anybody seen Honie Carlton?" I asked one the volunteers, who was distributing the next day's pairing sheets.

"I think somebody said she'd already headed off to Sarasota to get ready for next week," the woman answered.

I thought about that, frowning. Honie had not mentioned plans to head out of town early. And she hadn't said good-bye, which was not like her. I was trying to decide if my feelings were hurt, when my telephone chirped.

"Hacker? Karla Donnelly, Tour PR," said the well-modulated voice. "Mrs. Stilwell has some responses to the allegations in your story, and would like to give them to you."

"Fine," I said, getting out a piece of paper. "Shoot."

"No," the voice, said. "Please come to her suite. She will see you there."

"Aw, hell," I whined. "Can't you just read them? Save me a trip?"

"Ten minutes, Hacker," she said and rang off.

I groaned and swore silently to myself. I suspected that, surrounded by her courtesans, the Queen would have regained her powers, and that I would be in for some high-pressure browbeating. Part of me looked forward, perversely, to the challenge. The other part of me wished suddenly for a direct flight to the North Pole.

I drained the last of my can of beer, made an excellent over-the-head hook shot into the wastebasket beside the table, grabbed a notebook, and headed for the door.

"Night, Hacker," said Barley Raney as I departed. His head was still buried in the newspaper.

"Go home, Barley," I told him. "It's quittin' time."

"Yeah, right," he said.

The sun was fading fast in the western sky as I headed for

the main hotel building. The last few streaks of orange and pink fought a losing battle against the deep blue tones that were fading quickly into black. I stopped for a moment and watched the darkening gloom as it swept over the golf courses. The gushing fountain in the lake beside the eighteenth green made a comforting sound, like the wind rippling up a mountain pass, as the rest of the world seemed to hush suddenly from the bustle of the day. The pulsating buzz of insects slowed and even stopped for a beat or two. The lights of the city were twinkling on in the distance. The air was still and quiet, and at just the right temperature. The air had that quality that the zillions of tourists dreamed about when they thought about Florida, the quality that inspired the brochure writers. Redolent and peaceful and moist and full of sensuality. It made me think about Sybil Montgomery. It made me feel alive, even as the fall of death, of night, approached.

I breathed it in, and used it to fuel my resolve for what I was sure would be a bitter and acrimonious meeting with Big Wyn. Sighing, I turned and headed once again for the hotel.

Whoever got me was very good. I was, of course, not paying much attention to the immediate surroundings, but still, I never heard or saw a thing. I was just aware, suddenly, of a burst of pain at the base of my skull, an explosion of bright and multicolored lights, and the sensation of falling and falling end over end into a deep black eternity.

It took me a while to convince myself that I had returned from that eternity, because when I woke, I was still in a black, lightless void. Gradually, however, the dull throbbing of my head told me that I was, unfortunately, alive. My hands were tightly bound behind my back, and my shoulders chimed in with the message that they, too, hurt like hell. I would have groaned, but for the gag pulled tightly through my mouth and tied behind my head.

I figured out that I was in a smallish room. It was close and hot. It was so dark that I couldn't make out any distinguishing characteristics. I was sitting in a propped-up position on a hard daybed, my back uncomfortably wedged against the wall. The wall was cool and smooth and when I reached out as well as I could with my bound hands and touched it, there was a metallic texture to it, like a kitchen countertop.

I strained in the dark listening, trying to ignore the constant throbbing of my head. Nothing, except a rather constant buzz of insects. "Wherever I am, there's an outside nearby," I thought, and immediately credited myself with an amazing intuitive deduction. I struggled to sit up into a more comfortable position and discovered that my legs were hog-tied, too.

A wave of panic swept over me. Hands and feet tied, gagged, kept in the dark. "Okay, Commandant, I'll spill! Let me the hell out of here and I'll tell you anything you want to know. Just let . . . me . . . go!" Hot tears of frustration sprang up, a rush of fear-based adrenaline took over and drops of perspiration ran down my back. The noise made by my breathing in great draughts of frightened air through my nose reverberated in the small, hot room.

Slowly, I got myself back under control. "Easy, Hacker," I cautioned myself. "You are not dead, and if they wanted you dead, you would be by now. So relax, chill out, wait for the next act in this play to begin. All you've got left is your brain, so use it."

I don't know how long intermission was. I may have dozed off. I tried to let my mind just wander freely, to keep it off my current situation.

But I finally heard a soft whisper somewhere close at hand. Then a door opened beside me, spilling harsh light into my small room. Almost at once, I realized why the wall behind me was smooth and metallic. I was in a motor home, the back bedroom compartment. In front of me was a bed, the twin of the one I sat upon, extending almost the entire width of the trailer. There was a small window over the bed opposite me, tightly sealed with both blinds and curtains.

Sticking his head in the doorway, Harold Stilwell looked down at me and grunted.

"You're up, I see," he mumbled. "Sorry about the ropes and such. Wynnona said she needs to talk to you and make you listen to some reason."

180

I just looked at him. If I had been able to talk, I don't know what I would have said.

Stilwell went away, leaving the door open. Cooler air flooded my compartment, for which I was thankful. I didn't like the way I was beginning to smell. He was back in a few minutes.

"Listen," he said to me. "I don't know why y'all gotta be tied up like that, at least with that gag thingy. You could yell your fool head off out here, and nobody's hear a thing, 'cept maybe an alligator or two. Here, I brought you a beer. I'll take that thing out and help you drink it, and you promise to behave 'til Wynnona gets here. Deal?"

I nodded, and he reached behind me and untied the gag. When it came off, I worked my jaws up and down.

"Hear you go," Stilwell said, holding out a can of Budweiser. Like a baby with its pablum, I opened wide and swallowed the golden nectar of the gods. I can't remember when anything tasted so good to me. I probably emptied about half the can.

"Thanks," I gasped, finally.

"Don't mention it," Stilwell muttered, and took a draught of the can he had brought for himself.

"Harold, what the fuck is going on?" I said next.

He wiped his mouth with the back of his hand, then shook his head at me.

"Now, Hacker, don't get started with me," he cautioned. "I tole you, Wynnona needs to talk to you, and she said this was the only way to get you to listen. I don't like it much, but Big Wyn said it's gotta be this way."

"Big Wyn is wrong, Harold," I said. "This is called kidnapping and assault, and both you and Big Wyn can go to jail. I would listen to anything Big Wyn has to say to me, but this is called breaking the law."

He was silent, silhouetted in the light streaming in the door from the main body of the trailer. He took another long sip of his beer.

"What has she got on you, Stilwell?" I asked. "She catch you sleeping with a young rookie? She pay off the mortgage on

181

your gasoline station years ago? It's gotta be something like that."

"I don't know what you're talking about," Stilwell muttered.

"The hell you don't," I said. "That's the way Big Wyn works. She finds the weak link in everybody's life and then pushes on it until it breaks. And once it does, she owns you. Forever. That's how she's run this organization for the last twenty years. That's how she controlled Benton Bergmeister until she killed him. That's—"

"Wynnona Stilwell did not kill Benton Bergmeister!" Stilwell yelled and jumped up, spilling my beer. "She's a fine woman . . ."

"She's a witch, Harold," I said quietly. "She likes to run other people's lives. I don't know what she's got on you, but she runs your sorry life, too. The way she's always ordering you around, telling you what to do. Hell, she's even got you to be accessory to kidnapping! Don't tell me what a fine woman she is."

Harold Stilwell stood there in the doorway, breathing heavily. He drained the last of his beer and hurled the can against the wall of his trailer home.

"I'm tellin' you, Hacker, you've got it wrong," he said, his voice cracking with emotion.

I decided to give him one more push.

"Okay," I said. "If you insist on being dickless—"

My shove was one too many. With a strangled cry of fury, Stilwell sprang at me, grabbed me by the throat, and slammed my head backward, hard against that thin metal wall. The light in the small room swam around and around and my consciousness went swirling with it, down and down and out the drain.

CHAPTER 25

Asplash of cold water on my face pulled me up from the void this time. I opened my eyes and groaned against the harsh light. I had been moved, I quickly saw, into the larger compartment of the trailer, the combination living room/dinette, and plopped down on the built-in bench beside the small fold-down dining table. My head was resting on the hard, cold vinyl surface.

I groaned again and slowly raised my head, wincing in pain. My hands were still bound tightly behind my back, my legs tied at the ankles. I leaned back against the rest and looked around foggily. The light in the cabin was low, furnished by two small lamps. I could hear a generator chugging away outside the trailer.

Harold Stilwell stood over me, still holding the empty water glass which he had just dashed in my face. Standing over by the door was Big Wyn, looking at me with a combination of interest and hatred.

"Okay, Wyn, he's awake," Harold said. "I'm going outside and have a pipe." He fumbled in his coveralls for pipe and tobacco and went out the door into the night.

Wynnona Stilwell took two steps toward me and stood towering above me. I raised my eyes upward at a painful angle to look back at her. There was an unmistakable aura of conqueror and vanquished in the little cabin of Harold Stilwell's motor trailer. Big Wyn's eyes were bright and clear and shone with power. I imagined those eyes looked the same on those countless afternoons when she had marched down the eighteenth fairway with an insurmountable lead, cheers ringing in her ears.

"You have created more trouble than you're worth," Big Wyn said to me, her voice deep and sure. I looked at her more closely, and could not see the tired old woman I had spoken to earlier in the afternoon. Something had rejuvenated Wynnona Stilwell.

"You have stuck your nose into places you shouldn't have," she continued. "You have made my life most unpleasant. Normally, I could deal with that. There have been other reporters who have done slam pieces on our tour, even on me. Generally, I can ignore it. But you've gone too far, Hacker. You have endangered everything I have worked for over the last twenty years. I can't let you do that."

"I haven't done anything, Wyn," I said. "You created this house of horrors. Now you have to live with it. You are already in deep trouble, Wyn. Don't make it any worse for yourself. Cut the shit, let me go, and I'll tell the cops you came to your senses, no harm done."

She laughed at me. Threw back her head and laughed. A deep, throaty laugh tinged with madness. It sent a sudden chill down my back.

"Hacker, you don't know how much you sound like my father," she said. "He was such a spineless little bastard, but he always tried to sound like a big brave warrior. He tried to make us believe that he knew everything, had all the answers. But he didn't know anything about me. Hah!"

She looked at me with eyes that had turned suddenly hot and bright.

"I was supposed to be Daddy's little girl, do all the things little girls are supposed to do. Grow up, wear pretty dresses, get married, settle down, raise a family," she said. "That was his vision for me. I was a girl, after all, and that's what girls are supposed to do. He didn't give a damn about what I wanted, about how I felt. No, he had all the answers, and I was supposed to believe in them."

She began to pace in the cramped space of the camper. I didn't interrupt her, just listened.

"I knew I was different early on," she continued. "I knew I wanted more out of life. I found out early that I liked to compete. Even better, I liked to win. Especially against boys. But I could never make him understand. He wouldn't listen to me. He kept telling me I was just being silly, unladylike, that I'd understand once I settled down some."

She stopped pacing and looked at me. I saw an appeal for understanding in her eyes.

"But I was never a whole person for him, just a thing. He was always proud of my golfing achievements, but for him it was just like making the honor roll. 'That's fine,' he'd say, making it sound like something that would just occupy my time until the more important stuff came along."

Big Wyn laughed again, this time softly, ruefully.

"Then one day, after school, he came home and found me in bed with one of my friends, a girl I played golf with," she said. "I've realized since then that I got caught on purpose. It was the only way to make him understand that I was truly different than his dream of me."

She rubbed her thick hands wearily over her eyes.

"In any case, he dropped dead of a heart attack the next afternoon," she said quietly. "He just never understood me, never tried to understand."

I didn't reply. There was nothing I could think of to say. The sadness of Wynnona Stilwell's sorry life swept over me, followed quickly by a feeling of despair. I was the prisoner of an unbalanced woman, and I was in trouble.

"Anyway, Hacker, that's all in the past," Big Wyn said, her voice regaining the sharp edges it had earlier. "What's in the present is you and the trouble you've raised. I don't know what it is about you, Hacker. I've never had much trouble with the press boys before."

"How many have you had kidnapped and beaten up?" I wondered.

Big Wyn laughed. "Not too many," she said, chuckling. "Most of 'em just nuzzle up close enough for me to give 'em little bits of this and that and go off their own way. But you . . . you wouldn't do like you were told."

"Is that all this is, Wyn?" I said. "A power struggle? Does that justify things like beating up Honie Carlton?"

Big Wyn shook her head, frowning. "Well, now, I must say I didn't really approve of that," she said. "I just told Julie to go lean on the girl a little, make an impression. But Julie sometimes gets a little too excited trying to do what I tell her, 'cause she keeps hoping I'll sleep with her again. That was just one of those times." She laughed, a short, evil bray. "It's amazing what a little lust will do."

I shook my head in wonder.

"And what about Benton Bergmeister?" I asked. "He told me he was going to walk out of your little circus here, and I suspect he was going to blow a few whistles on your operation. Isn't it nice that he accidently ingested the wrong pills the other night?"

Big Wyn shrugged, evading my eyes. "Accidents will happen," she mumbled.

"I don't suppose the lovely Casey Carlyle had anything to do with that, did she?" I asked.

Big Wyn spun on me. "How did you know that?" she blurted out, then halted abruptly, realizing what she had just admitted.

"Two plus two, Wyn," I said. "I know she's the general errand girl around here, as well as your undercover agent. It makes sense that if Benton needed a refill on his prescriptions, he'd call Casey to go do it for him. The way I figure it, she went and got his prescription filled, plus one for herself for a big bottle of Nembutal. I checked with the medical examiner. Both Nembutal and Minizide come in capsules *and* they are almost identical in appearance, especially if the patient is usually too drunk to see. So, on the way back, Casey just switched the pills in the bottles and gave Benton his prescription bottle, containing a prescription for death."

"You can't prove that, Hacker," Wyn said fiercely.

"Maybe so, maybe not," I said. "But the cops are checking the area drugstores, and they'll discover that it was Casey who had the prescription filled. I figure they'll haul her lovely ass in for some serious questioning. Won't look good, Wyn, not good at all."

The door to the trailer suddenly swept open, and Honie Carlton was pushed inside. She too was tied, hands behind back, and a gag was fixed firmly through her lips. She looked at me with wide, frightened eyes, and moaned softly. Coming in behind her, a vicious smile creasing her face, was Julie Warren, and behind her doddered Harold Stilwell, his eyes big and round.

Honie was maneuvered into the bench across the table from me. The girl was sick with fear, and when she sat down, I could see the beginnings of fresh bruises on her face, and a trickle of blood at the corner of her mouth.

"Goddamnit!" I yelled at Big Wyn. "If you dare lay another hand on this girl, I'll have you in jail for the rest of your sorry life!"

Big Wyn laughed again and backhanded me with a solid swing of her meaty hand. My head rocked back against the seat rest, and I gasped at the sudden, stinging pain. Moments later, I felt the blood run out of my nose and down my cheeks, until it began to drip onto my shirt. Honie saw the blood and moaned softly again.

I stared at Big Wyn, studying her through the pain. Her eyes were aglow, her nostrils flared with pleasure. I decided that Wynnona Stilwell was truly a sick person.

"Here now." Harold Stilwell finally found his voice. "There's no cause for that, Wynnona," he remonstrated. "You said you just wanted to talk to this here fella. There was nothing said about—"

Big Wyn turned furiously and spat her words out. "You

187

shut the hell up, Hal. Just shut up! When I want to hear some goddamn thing from you I will ask. Until then, shut up!"

Big Wyn locked eyes with her husband. Whatever it was he saw there, it caused him to sit back down and shut up.

"Wyn," I rasped, "this has gone far enough. You can't believe you'll get away with anything. The story will come out anyway. Barley Raney—"

"Barley Raney will do what I tell him," Big Wyn asserted. "We know that you haven't transmitted your story to Boston yet. We also know you work alone. So we'll take our chances that when you're out of the picture, the story dies."

"And how are you gonna get me out of the picture?" I asked, not really wanting to know the answer.

Big Wyn merely smiled her nasty little smile. She wheeled, opened the door to a closet in the bedroom wall, and reached inside. Turning, she held in her hands a shotgun, an over/ under Remington .365, it looked like. Honie Carlton moaned again when she saw it. I wanted to moan but stifled the urge. Moaning is not manly.

"The story will be that horny ole Hacker here ran off with one of our young assistant publicity officers," Big Wyn said. "You see, they were old and dear friends, but Miss Carlton grew up in the nicest ways all of a sudden, and Hacker just had to have it. So off they go. Probably screwin' their way around the Caribbean or somethin'. You're on vacation, aren't you Hacker? So you won't be missed for a few weeks. And we'll have a hastily written letter from Miss Carlton here, resigning her job all of a sudden for personal reasons. It'll play. People'll snicker and then forget all about it."

"God, that's brilliant," Julie Warren breathed.

Harold Stilwell cleared his throat. "Uh, Wynnona, I'm not sure I understand . . ."

"Oh you understand all right," Big Wyn said sarcastically. "You know exactly what's goin' on here. So here—" She handed him the shotgun. "Take 'em out and kill 'em and make sure they go into a lagoon with a couple of hungry gators. Don't want any bodies comin' back later."

Harold Stilwell took the gun and stared at it for a moment.

Then, sitting on his camp chair, he looked beseechingly up at his wife.

"Wyn, honey, I can't—"

"Harold Stilwell," Big Wyn thundered, "you will do as I say. I have spent the last twenty years taking care of your sorry ass. Everything you've got in this world I gave you. The food you eat, the clothes on your back, even this godforsaken piece of trash you live in . . . they are all mine. I earned the goddamn money all these years. All you have ever been good for is doing what I tell you. I own you, Harold Stilwell—lock, stock, and barrel—and you know it. If it wasn't for me, you'd still be a dumb hick running a gas station in Nowhere, Indiana! So quit beatin' around the bush and whinin' and do as I say."

His eyes teared, and he ducked his head in shame. "Wyn—" He stammered, "D-d-don't make me . . ."

"Goddamn it," she yelled back, bending down low over him, getting right in his face. "Did you hear what I just said? Without me, you are a worthless worm! Do you hear me? Worthless! I'm not going to tell you again. Now do it, god-damn it, DO IT!"

Harold Stilwell sat up as if stuck by lightning. His eyes were still wet, but he glanced down and jacked a shell into the chamber. The authoritative click of that shell ramming home sounded a lot like a death knell to me.

Suddenly, the gun roared. Instinctively, I flinched and ducked, and I saw Honie, across the table, jump reflexively at the sound.

Harold Stilwell, still sitting on his little camp chair, held the shotgun pointed at the ample midsection of his wife. She was looking at him with a puzzled expression on her face. She stood there, unmoving, for a long moment, while the smell of cordite filled the trailer, and the sound of the shotgun blast reverberated. Then, as if in slow motion, she crumpled, word-less, to the floor.

Julie Warren, who had been standing and grinning quietly against the far wall, sprang forward with a cry.

"What the—! Wyn . . . WYN?" She pulled Big Wyn over on her back. Her midsection was a mass of splattered blood.

189

"You killed her!" Julie yelled furiously at Harold, spit spraying from her mouth. "You killed her! Goddamn it . . . you . . . "

She took half a step toward the old man sitting on his chair. The gun roared a second time, and Julie Warren's face disintegrated in a horrifying spray of red. The ceiling, the wall, and Honie Carlton and I were misted with blood and tissue from Julie Warren's exploding head. As her lifeless body tumbled over backward, I fought down the bile that rose quickly in my throat. Across the table, Honie Carlton whimpered once and fainted.

Only now did Harold Stilwell move. Slowly, as if bothered by arthritis, he eased out of his camp chair, holding the shotgun in front of him. He stepped daintily over the two bodies at his feet and ambled to a storage closet along the far wall. He pulled the door open, reached inside, and came out with a handful of fresh shells.

"No, Harold, don't," I begged. "There's been enough killing."

If he heard me, he didn't react. He calmly broke the shotgun open, popped out the spent, smoking shells, and thumbed two fresh rounds into the magazine. He clicked the gun closed again and pumped them into the chamber. Slowly he turned, the gun pointing out, until he was facing me.

"Harold, please," I begged. "Shoot me if you have to, but she's just an innocent bystander. Please don't."

Harold Stilwell never spoke a word. His eyes were gray and dead and empty. He raised the gun in his arms, then turned it around with his hands until the barrel was tucked underneath his own chin.

"No!" I yelled frantically. "No! No! No!"

The gun roared for a third and final time.

CHAPTER 26

It was midmorning before someone showed up. It was Charley Dillon, the Doral's maintenance man, coming to find Harold Stilwell, probably to share a coffee break with his old pal, talk about great engines they had known. He found his old pal mostly faceless and splattered against the wall of his trailer.

He also found two other bodies and a semiconscious Honie Carlton. She had awakened, wept, moaned softly, and then gone catatonic—no doubt in shock. I was sitting calmly, hands bound, on my bench.

"Good morning," I said when the guy stuck his horrified head in the door and took all this in. "I'd appreciate it if you would first untie my hands and then get on the horn and call the cops."

He untied my hands second. First he blew his breakfast all over the ground outside the trailer.

I figured it had been five, maybe six hours that I had been sitting there alone in the trailer. Five, six hours with three dead people, and one young and innocent victim. Five, six hours

191

with lots of graphic things to look at. Lots of time to think about things. Like evil. Unhappiness. Life and death.

Strangely, perhaps, I found myself thinking more about Harold Stilwell than his famous wife. I knew that Big Wyn's story would get the most play in the media: the famous golfing star blown away by her deranged husband. Tragedy on the links! One of America's heroes meets her doom. I could hear Jack Whitaker doing one of his wordy essays on the tube, waxing poetic about "Death be not proud" or some such nonsense.

No, Wynnona's story was not interesting to me, sitting there that night and morning in the trailer of death. There are hundreds of Big Wyn's in this day and age. Oh, they might not be sports stars and media darlings, and they usually don't end up lying crumpled in a bloody heap . . . but they are out there. They are the businessmen who like to manage using fear as the primary motivational tool. They are the husbands and wives who enact some measure of revenge against the helplessness of living in the modern world by making miserable the lives of those close at hand. They are the pool-hall bullies with the meaty fists and the college professors with the snippy repartee. They are all those who are not happy unless the world is remade to their liking, and that's such an impossible job that they are rarely happy.

No, I spent those five or six hours thinking about Harold, the little guy who suddenly had enough. That doesn't happen often enough. The little guys in our world get used to taking abuse, putting up with the bullying, making the best of it, shrugging the shoulder, and putting the best foot forward.

Like most of the little guys in the world, Harold Stilwell did not demand much: peace and quiet, some time to do some fishing, a little respect. But even those small demands are too much for the Big Wyn's of the world, who are threatened by any demand which does not originate with or have a direct bearing on themselves.

Harold's part of the story would never play, I knew. The little guys are rarely, if ever, heard. That's why they're the little guys. He would be remembered as the crazy guy who blew away that famous golfing lady. Not as a man abused for years who finally had enough and did something, even a drastic something, about it.

It was indeed all a bunch of mumbo jumbo. I remembered that phrase, sitting there amid the expired lives oozing blood onto the floor of Harold Stilwell's trailer. *A bunch a damn mumbo jumbo.* It's what Hal had said when I had tried to gently suggest to him that he didn't need to live his life under Big Wyn's thumb. It was what Big Wyn had said when she realized that her house of cards was about to come crashing down.

It was, I thought to myself while I spent five or six hours watching three bodies cool, a perfect summation of what life is all about. *A bunch a damn mumbo jumbo.*

I felt very badly about Harold Stilwell, and for all the other guys like him in this world. It stayed with me for the next day or so, while I was floating in and out of interviews with the police and the media and the police again. I kept all this stuff to myself, bottled up inside, and instead simply reported the events that had occurred. I just did my job.

The headlines were screamers, including the one over the story I wrote and filed with my editor in Boston. He thought it was good enough to copyright. I think I heard him mumble something about a Pulitzer, but I told him that was all a bunch a damn mumbo jumbo.

It was a pretty factual account. I never once mentioned anything about little guys having taken about as much as they could take.

The final round of the tournament was cancelled immediately, and for a few hours, the future of the Ladies' Professional Golf Association Tour was in some doubt. First the commissioner and then the players' committee president had died, unleashing a flood tide of scandal and rumor. Honie Carlton was treated for shock and recovered. Casey Carlyle was arrested as an accessory to murder. The networks wanted me to relate the events of that night in Harold Stilwell's trailer. So did the gossip tabloids. Since I never could tell the difference between the two, I declined to be interviewed by either.

193

But Monday morning, as I was packing in my hotel room and beginning to think longingly of my tiny beach cabin atop the bluff, the telephone rang. It was Mary Beth Burke.

"Hacker," she said, "some of the girls and I have been meeting, and we've reached some decisions and we want you to be the first to hear them. Can you come down to the conference room?"

I went. I figured the immediate prospects for the Tour were pretty bleak. Sponsors would no doubt withdraw in droves, clubs would cancel tournaments, and the TV boys would be running hellbent for the hills. Controversy may sell tickets, but scandal spells death. The LPGA could expect excellent press coverage from the supermarket tabloids for the next several months.

In the meeting room were most of the big-name girls on Tour: Patty Sheehan, Betsy King, Rosie Jones, Nancy Lopez, Pat Bradley, along with a handful of others, and Mary Beth Burke and Sybil Montgomery. Burkey seemed to be the spokeswoman for the group, which regarded me with interest and curiosity when I walked into the room.

"Hacker," Burkey said when I sat down, "we've been having a real cat fight in here for the last coupla hours, but we've scratched it out and come to some agreements."

I looked around the table. I could see on the faces of the golfers there that the discussion had been candid and brutal.

"We all agree that the one thing that's most important to us is that we keep on playin' golf," Burkey continued. "All of us in here, and I think just about every girl on tour, agree that playin' the game is what we're all about. The money, the glory, the fame and fortune stuff is all well and good, but it ain't worth shit if you can't play the game."

She looked around the table, gathering strength from the nods of agreement.

"Now, we ain't stupid, and we know that there's an awful long road ahead of us," Burkey said. "We're gonna lose sponsors, we're gonna lose tournaments, we're gonna lose TV money . . . hell, even the golf-ball people might not give us range balls!"

194

There was laughter.

"But what we've agreed here this morning is that we don't give a shit!" Mary Beth Burke raised her voice emphatically. "We're gonna dig our damn heels in the dirt and keep on playin'! If it turns out we end up playin' for a hundred dollars first-place money in some dohicket muni course in front of seven people, three kids, and a dog, well, we're damn well gonna do it. Because that's what's important . . . playin' the game. We figure once the people realize we're serious, they'll come back."

Mary Beth looked around the conference table once more.

"This time around, we're gonna run this show the right way," she continued. "Everyone in this room is gonna be responsible. And we have done held an election and our little ole British princess here has been officially elected and sworn in as the new head bitch!"

Sybil gazed at me with eyes bright and alive and proud.

"So that's about it," Burkey finished up. "We just wanted you to hear about all this because of what you had to go through and all, and we just hope that you'll see fit to give us another chance to prove ourselves some point down the road."

It was my turn to study the faces sitting around the table. I liked what I saw. There was resolve and determination and pluckiness. There was also the peace and new-found power that belongs only to the little guys who decide to stop being little guys.

I stood up.

"When you get things straightened out and put on your first tournament, call me," I said. "I'll be there." I paused. "And I'll even pay my own way!"

They hooted and laughed as I walked out and headed for home.